Little Stories from the House of Maxwell

The Adventures
of
Smitty Gumshoe

These Stories are Dedicated to the Kids, and Those Who are Still Kids at Heart.

Stories by Larry L. Maxwell

Artwork by Frankie A. Maxwell

The Adventures of Smitty Gumshoe – Puck-A-Gin; Mitty; Mud Dobber's Delight; Mildred the Moo; Arrow of Stone; Wampus Kitty

Written by Larry L. Maxwell

Illustrations and Artwork by Frankie A. Maxwell

Copyright © 2019 by Larry L. Maxwell; United States Library of Congress

All rights reserved. No part of this publication may be reproduced, stored in a retrieval system, or transmitted in any form or by any means – for example; electronic, photocopy, recording, etc. – without the prior written permission of the publisher.

ISBN: 9781797563244

Cover Illustration & Artwork by Frankie A. Maxwell

Editing by F. Matt Hogle

*The pages of these books have been reproduced from all original handpainted plates by Frankie A. Maxwell.

Table of Contents

Puck-A-Gin - Page 1

Mitty - Page 21

Mud Dobber's Delight - Page 45

Mildred The Moo - Page 75

Arrow Of Stone - Page 95

Wampus Kitty - Page 115

iv

PUCK-A-GIN

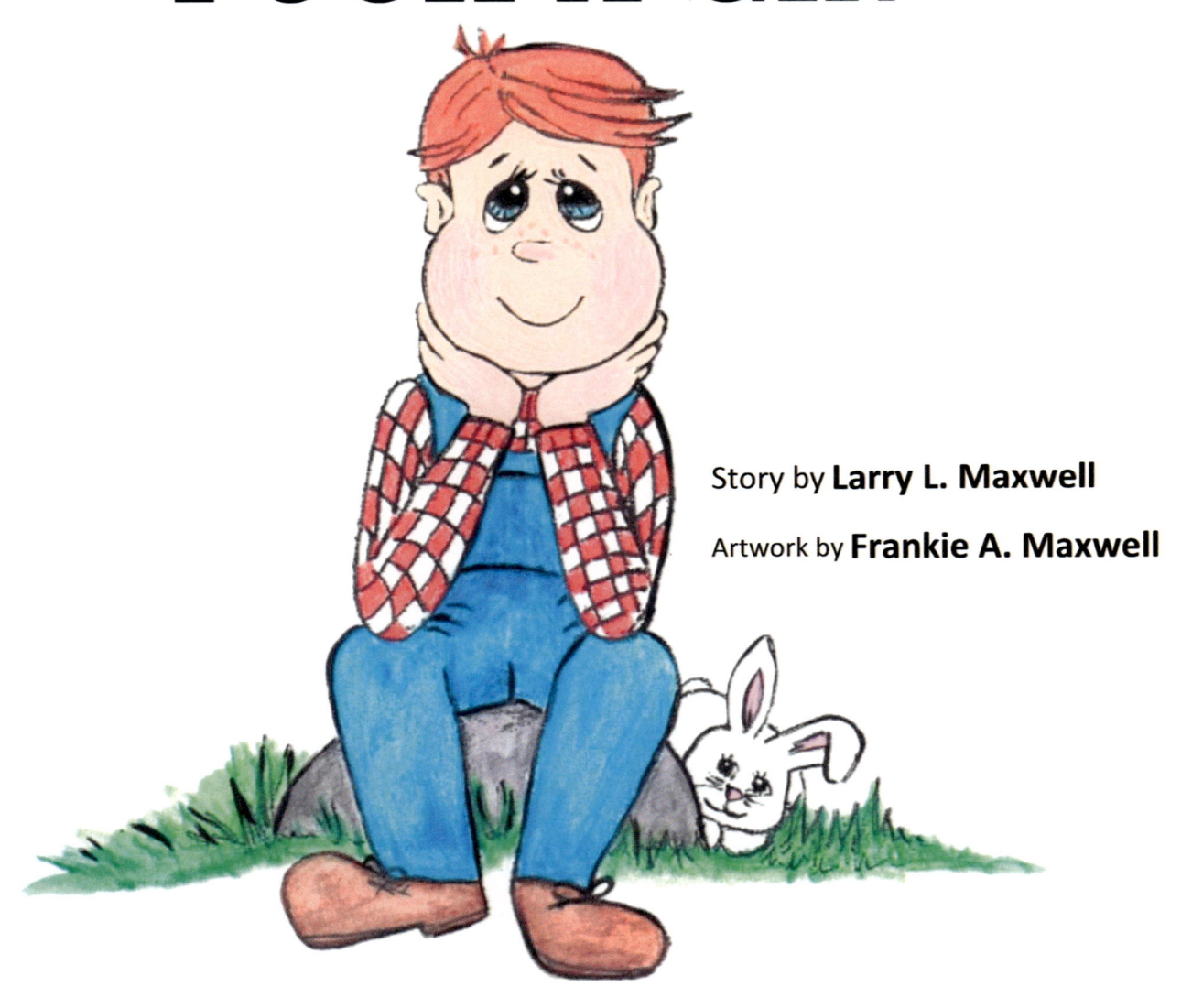

Story by **Larry L. Maxwell**

Artwork by **Frankie A. Maxwell**

Now Smitty Gumshoe, as most boys do, he liked to roam. His dad says its ok, but not to far from home.

4

Yet time and again - it seemed without ending each trip seemed a little longer from now to beginning

It was on one such trip to the highlands he'd go. Up closer to the mountain tops, and winter's white snow.

In one of his travels he was almost afright.
It was there that he saw this unusual sight!

Here was another little guy, just about his size. With long straight black hair, and dark, dark eyes. He didn't have much clothes, not like little Smitty. He had feet for shoes, a red color quite pretty.

His head was wrapped up and a feather was there. It kinda seemed strange - stuck, up in his hair.

Hi there! Hello! My name is Smitty. He didn't say much, guess he wasn't quite ready. And then when I thought the silence won't end.

A quiet voice from this shy little guy, "Me Puck-A-Gin". This was to be the way of his Indian Friend. In his shy little way, About all he could say was "Puck-A-Gin".

Now Smitty had heard that Indians don't talk much, But it really wasn't important - this talking and such

They laughed and they played on each opportune day, Smitty talked for them both as they continued to play.

Sometimes they would go hunting along the game trails. Each had his own way of his story to tell. As Smitty would look and get so excited. You could tell at a glance that Puck-A-Gin was delighted.

He mumbled a little and motioned a lot. I guess that was some kinda special Indian talk.

They would track the wild animals that might do them harm. One day they even tracked the milkcow right up to the barn. They couldn't figure it out as they looked front and back. But sure enough there she was standing right in those tracks.

Then they would both laugh at their joke, as each gave a nudge or an innocent poke.

"I guess that's all right", Smitty said with a grin. When you've got a great scout like my friend Puck-A-Gin.

Sometimes they would sit by the big river's bend. And try to say names, over and over again.

Puck-A-Gin's face would draw up real tight, as he made quite a sight and try to say Smitty, with all of his might. He would twist, then fidget, then scratch his chin, He hardly would know how his name would begin.

Finally he said it, it wasn't real pretty. With a great deal of effort, he finally said, "Mitty." "Say it again! Say it again!" shouted his friend Smitty. So with a shout! He let it all out, "Mitty! Mitty!"

The End

Mitty

Story by Larry L. Maxwell

Artwork by Frankie A. Maxwell

Now Puck-A-Gin lived in a Hogan way up near the sky. I guess Indians liked looking down, he didn't know why.

His father was brave and a great hunter too.

He told the great stories, and the bad bear he once slew.

His ears were all hearing, his eyes ever seeing.

As Puck-A-Gin thought that's what I want being.

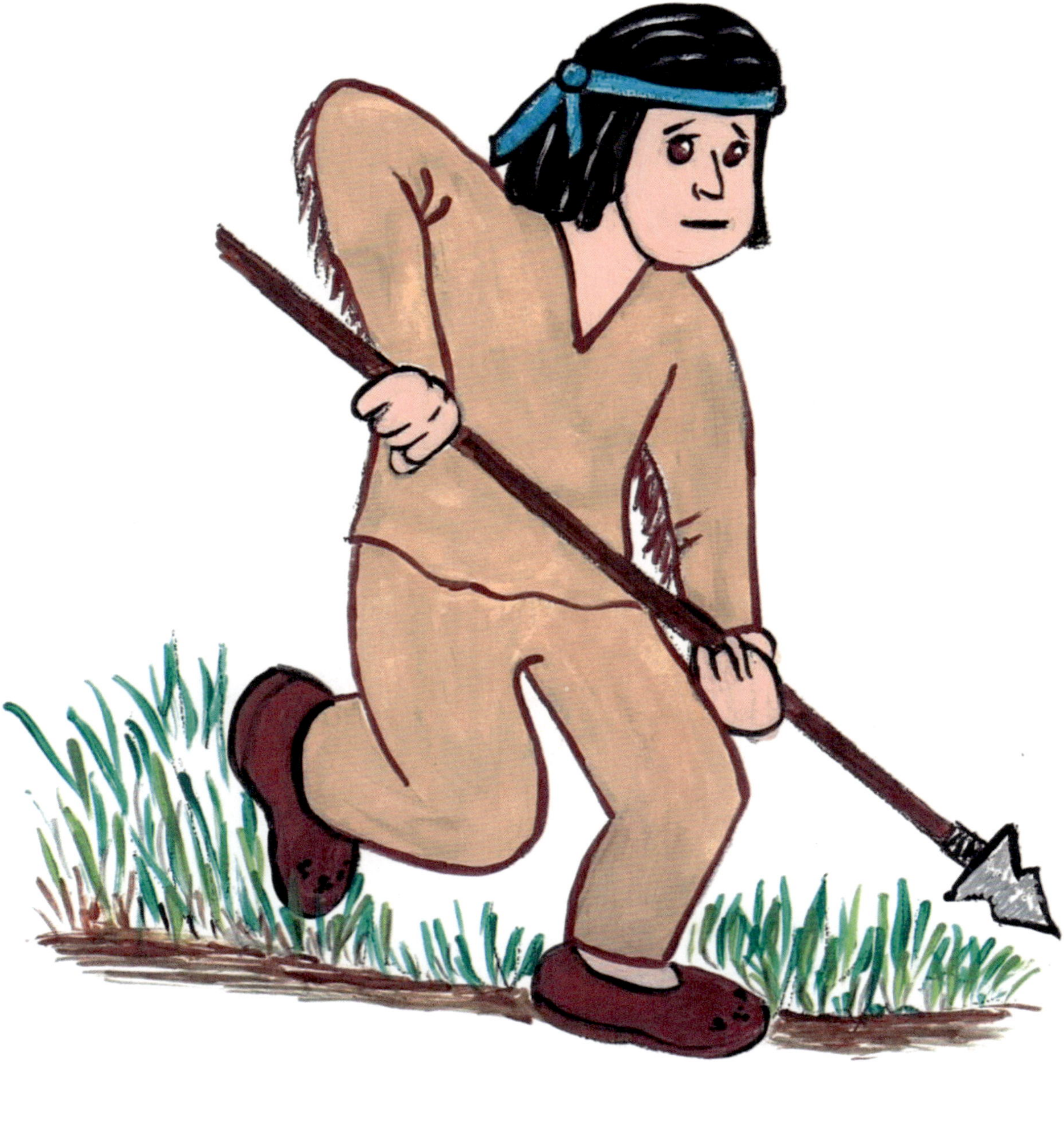

With arrow and bow, and a sharp hatchet too.

There just probably wasn't anything his dad couldn't do.

For sure he was a great hunter.

He brought home the meat.

And Nuk-A-Chuck his dad brought plenty to eat.

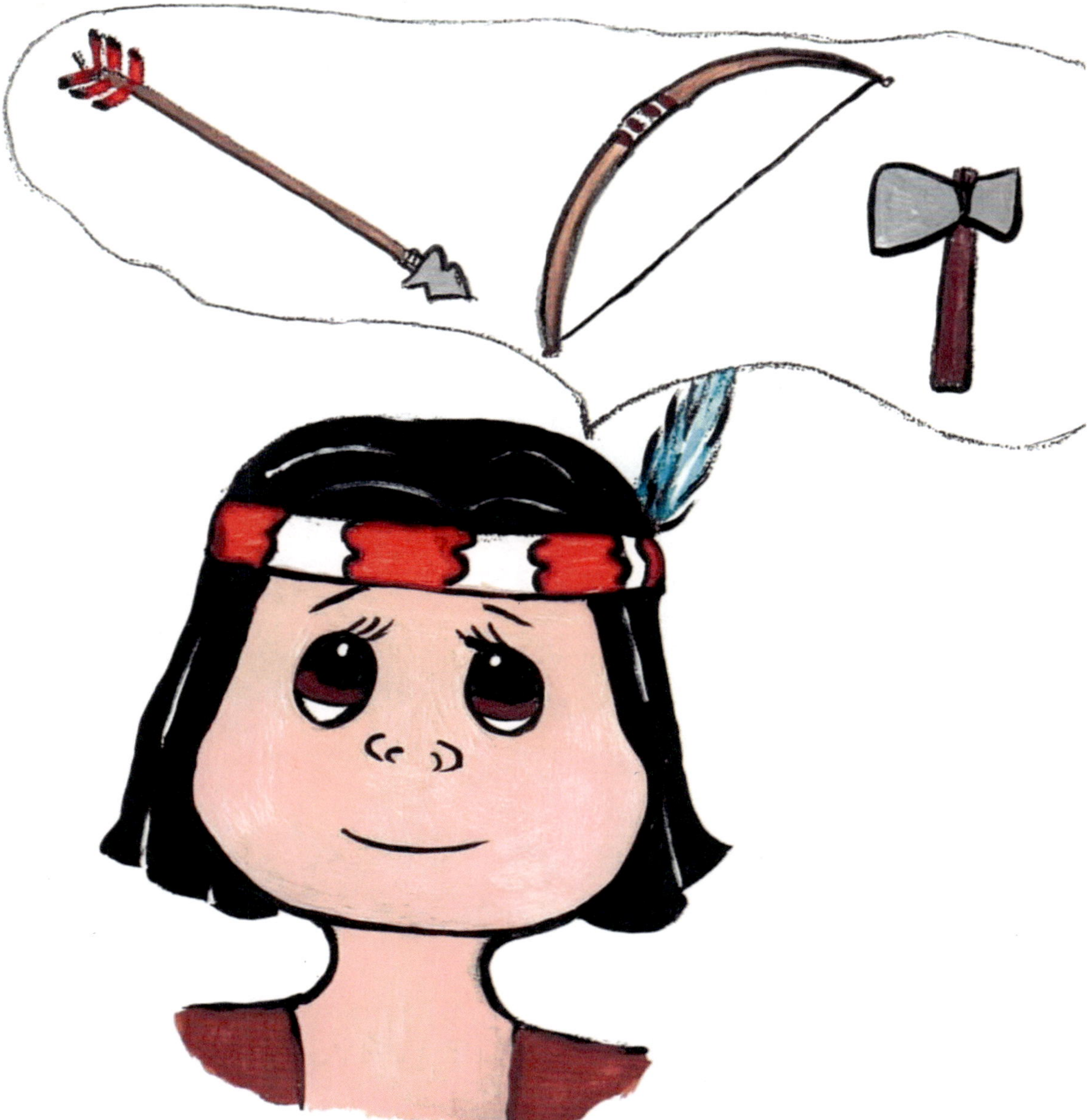

He would show him the ways, and signs, again, and again.Tell it pretty well wore me out, me, Puck-A-Gin

It was on such a venture, I slipped down below. There was always some special place I needed to go.

Then on one such day, I found this great sight

I heard something coming – It was a white boy alright.

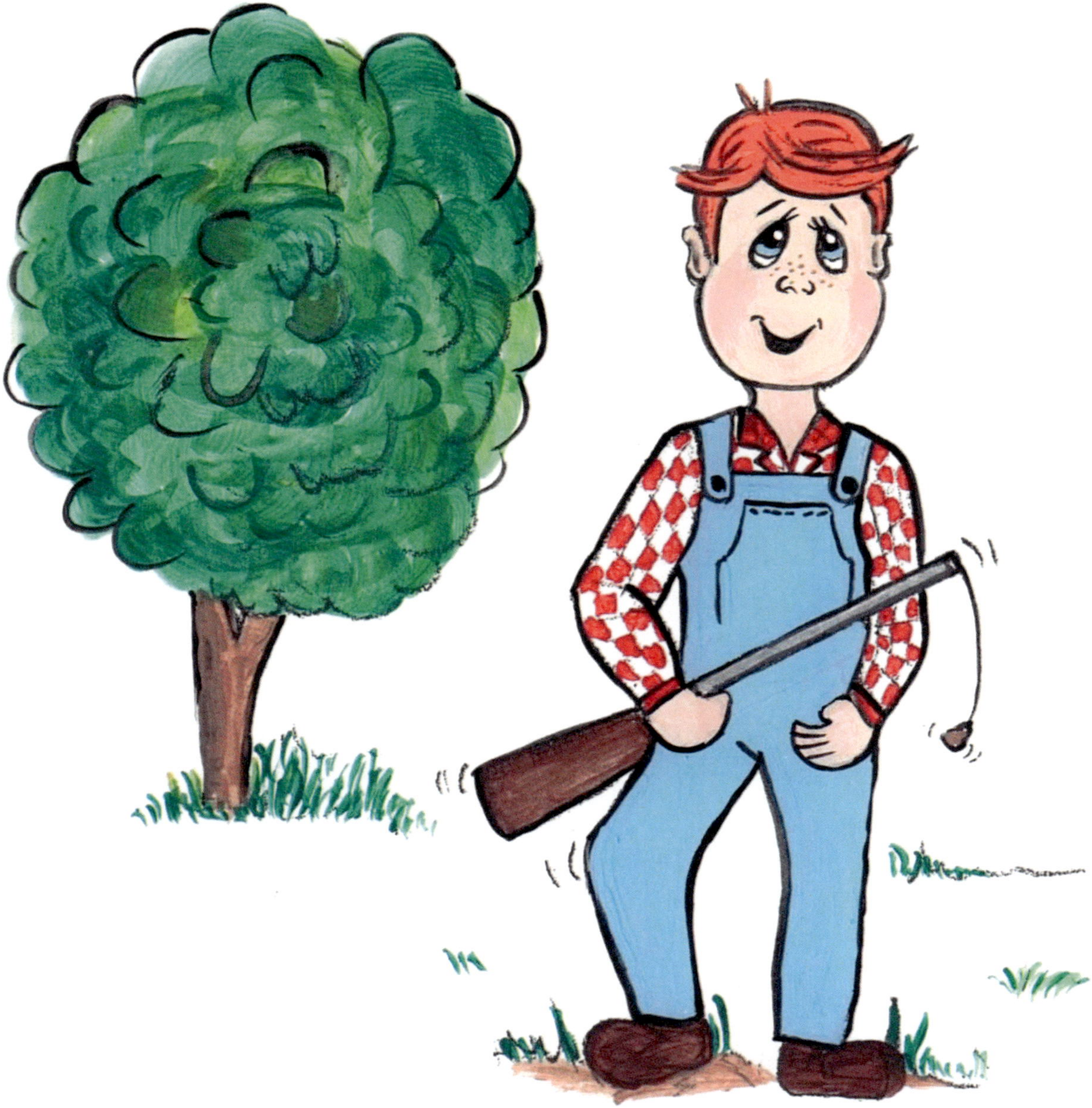

He talked kind of funny, And looked funny too.

I just listened and watched. Now what should I do?

Us Indians, well I guess we're quite proud. And usually real quick, not used to speaking so loud.

But this friendly boy seemed ok to me.

I just watched and stood still as quiet as can be.

Boy! How white kids can talk, all that white boy stuff.

I just listened and watched til he'd talked enough.

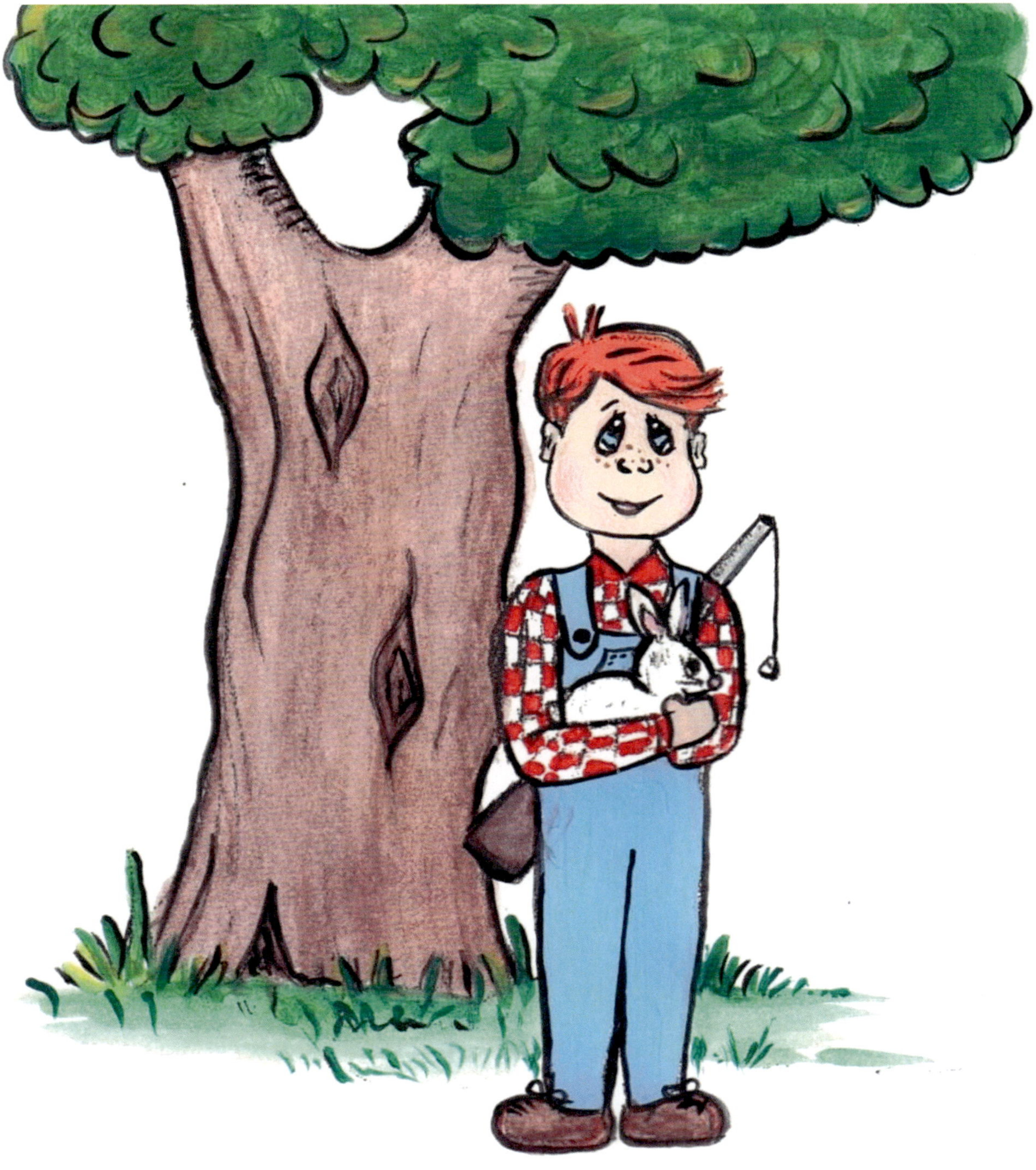

When he asked me my name, I said, "I Puck-A-Gin"

He looked kind of surprised that my silence would end.

Then he tried to get me to say Smitty.

Me, Puck-A-Gin.

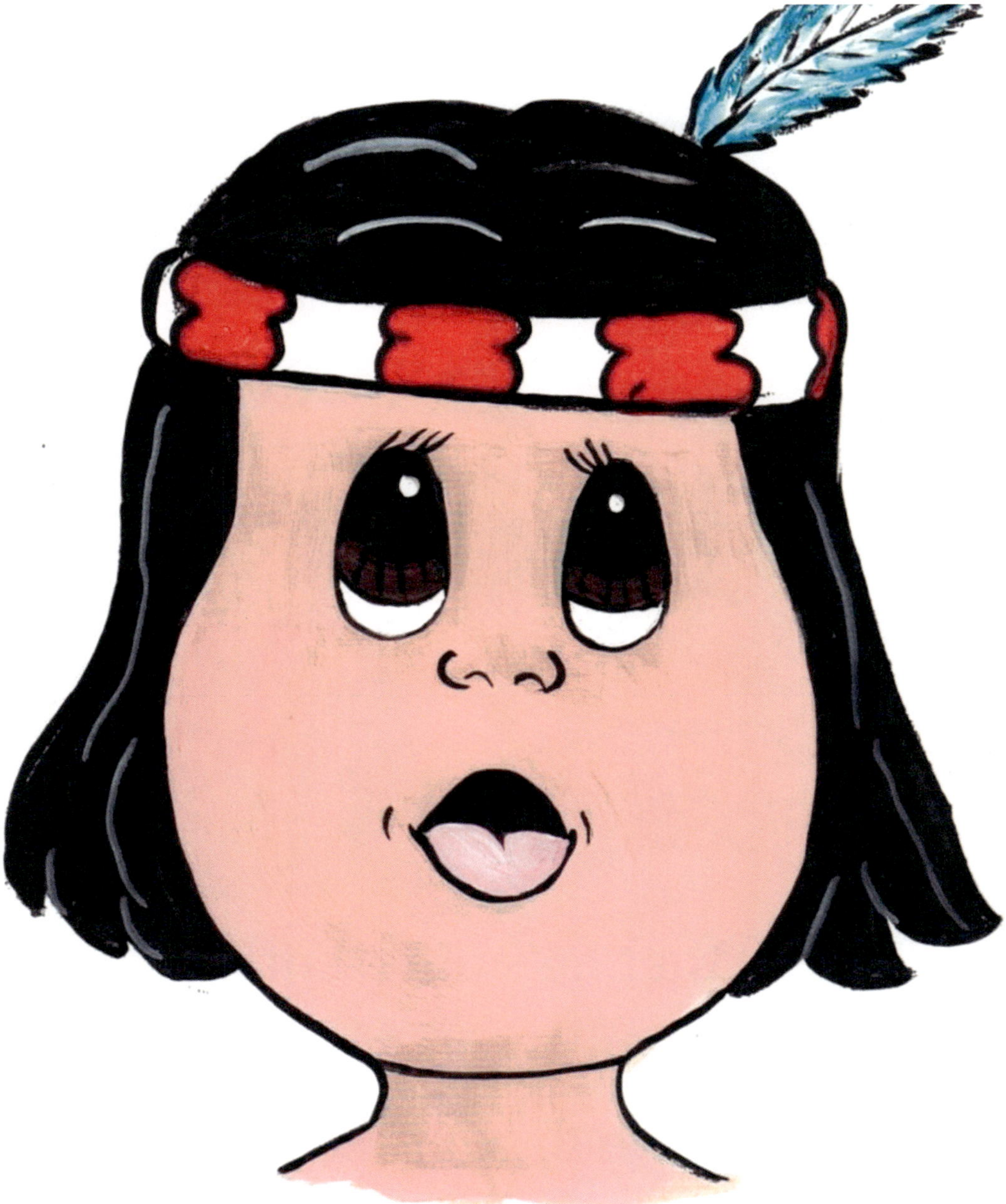

I know that he's different, my friend they call Smitty.

With clear blue water eyes, and hair that's quite pretty.

I know that he likes me, I like him a lot.

Now, How say his name? I nearly forgot.

Oh Yeah! Mitty the fire haired top.

It's real hard to say, and hard to get ready.

But I'll try it again, "Mitty, Mitty, Mitty."

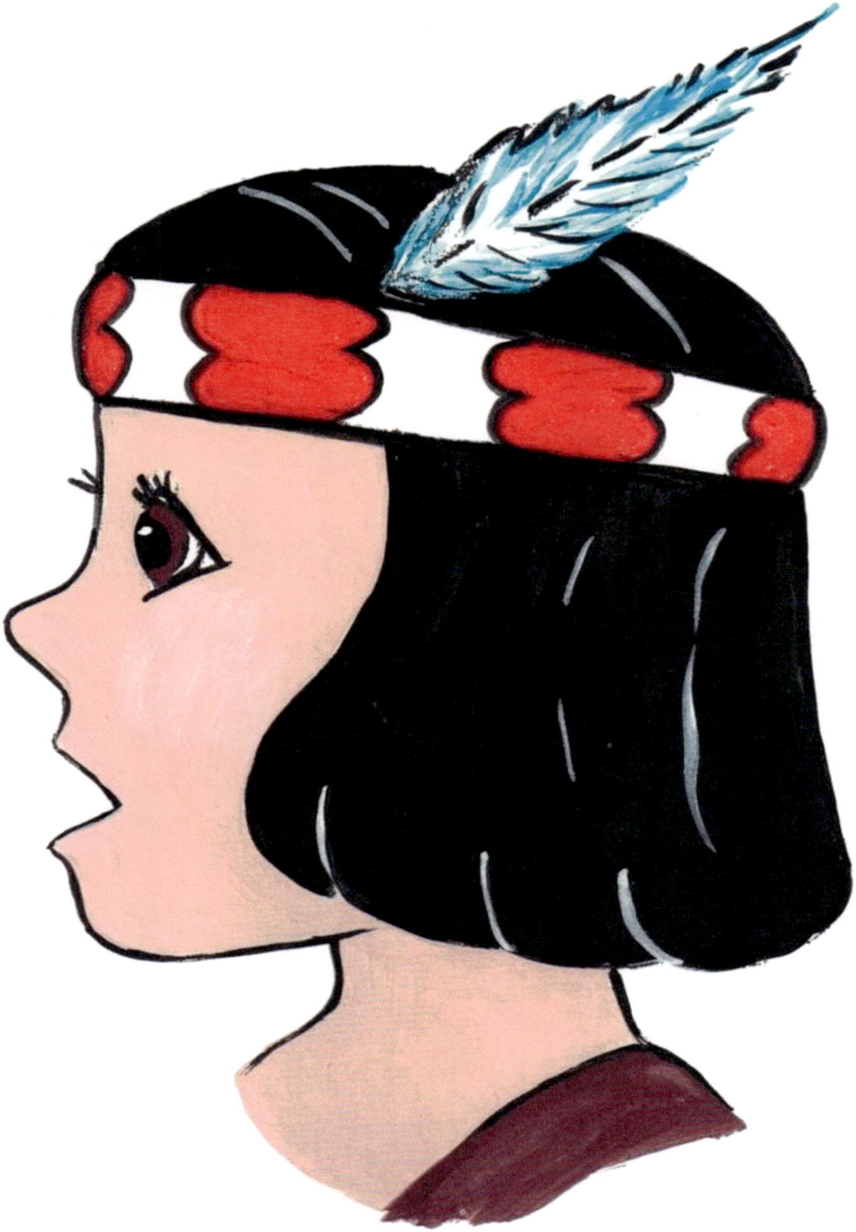

The End

Mud Dobber's Delight

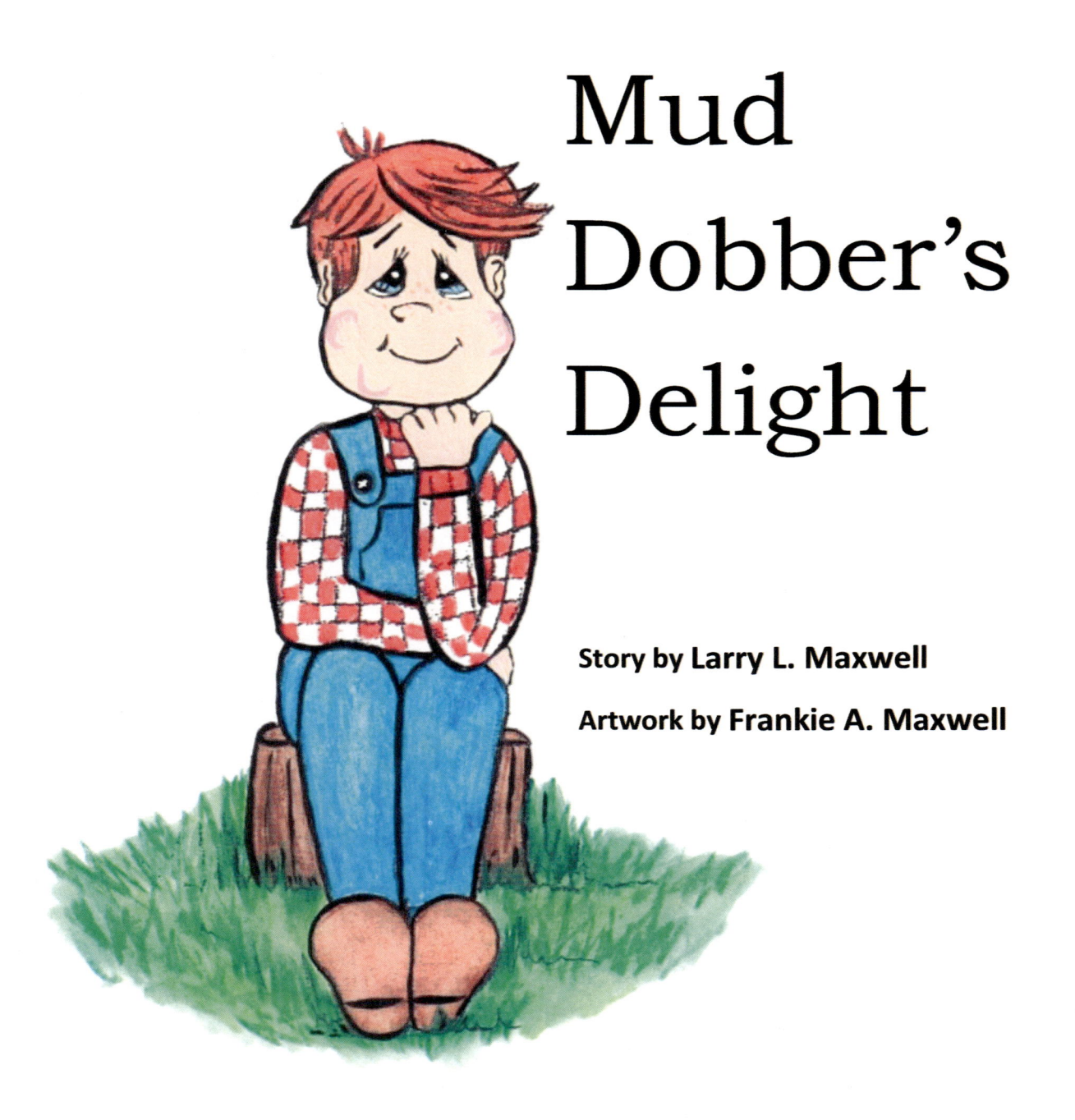

Story by Larry L. Maxwell

Artwork by Frankie A. Maxwell

You know it's just great, Smitty thought with a grin.

I've got this plan today, for me and Puck-A-Gin.

You see I've been giving some things lot's of thought.

And yet I don't know whether this plans any good or not.

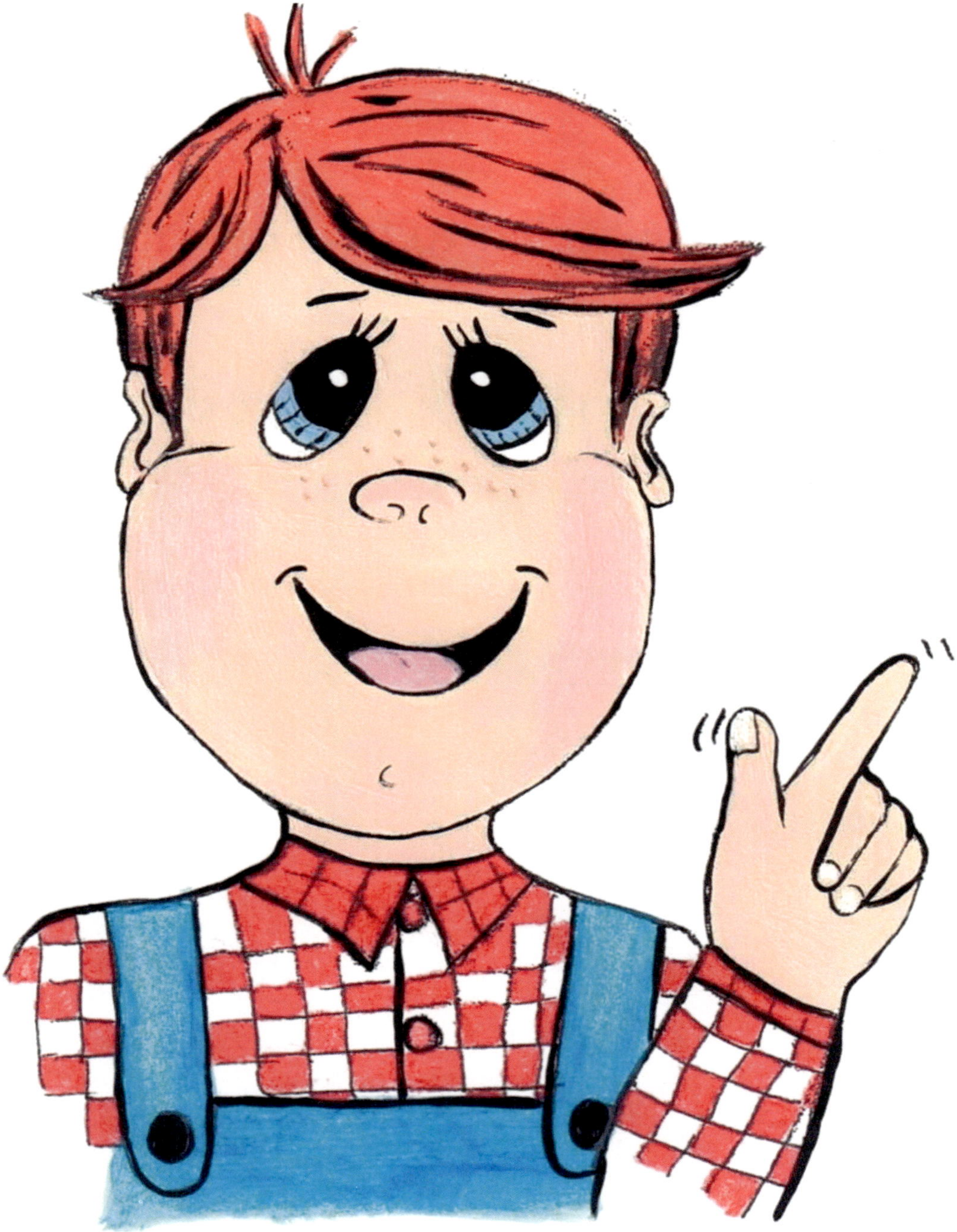

But I will tell it to my special Indian friend.

And try to read his hand signs, again, and again.

In my best thinking, I wonder where honey bees go?

Maybe we would follow them, and then we would know.

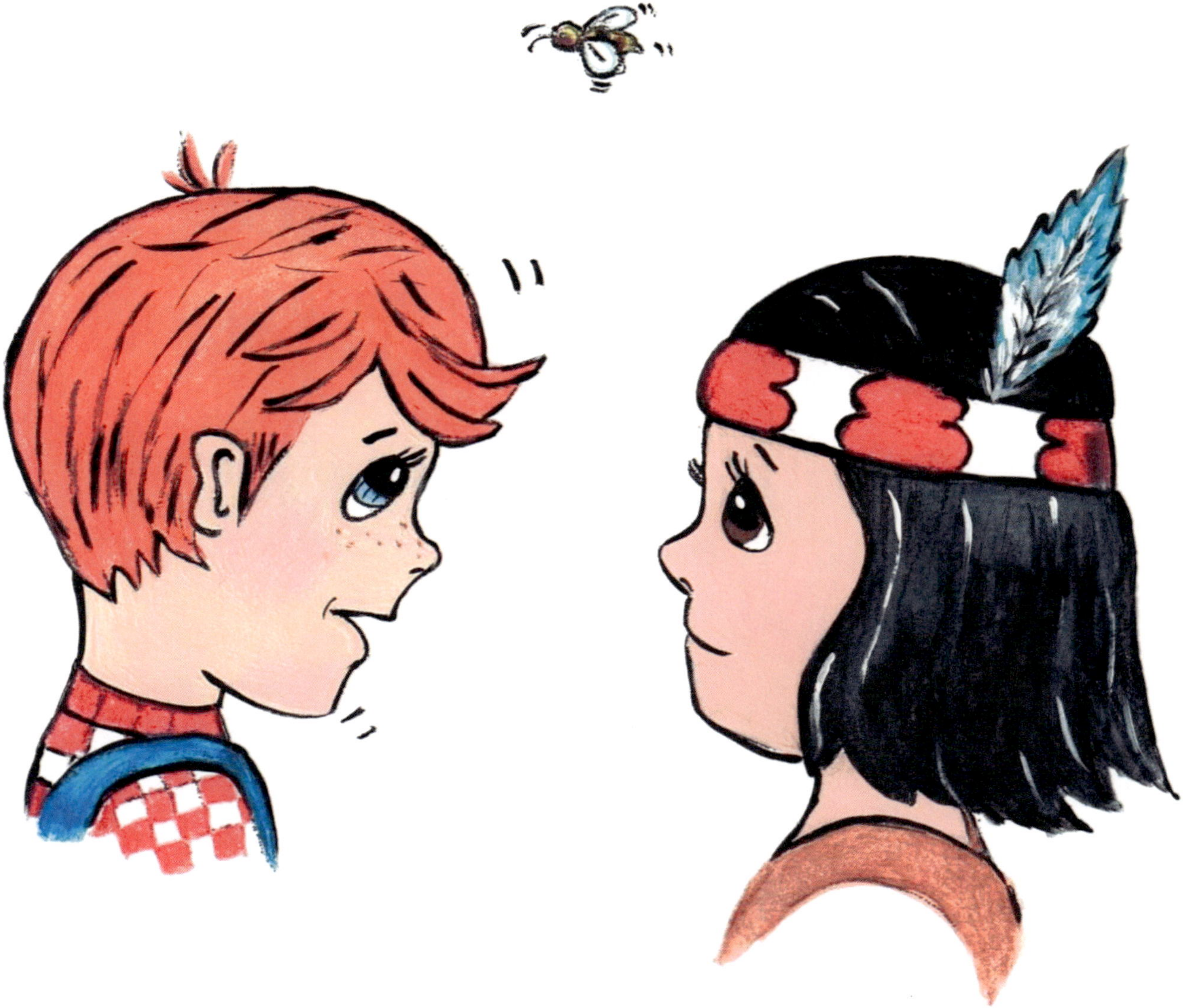

Dad says, "They make that honey, that is real nice and sweet."

Boy! I'd bet Puck-A-Gin would like a little to eat.

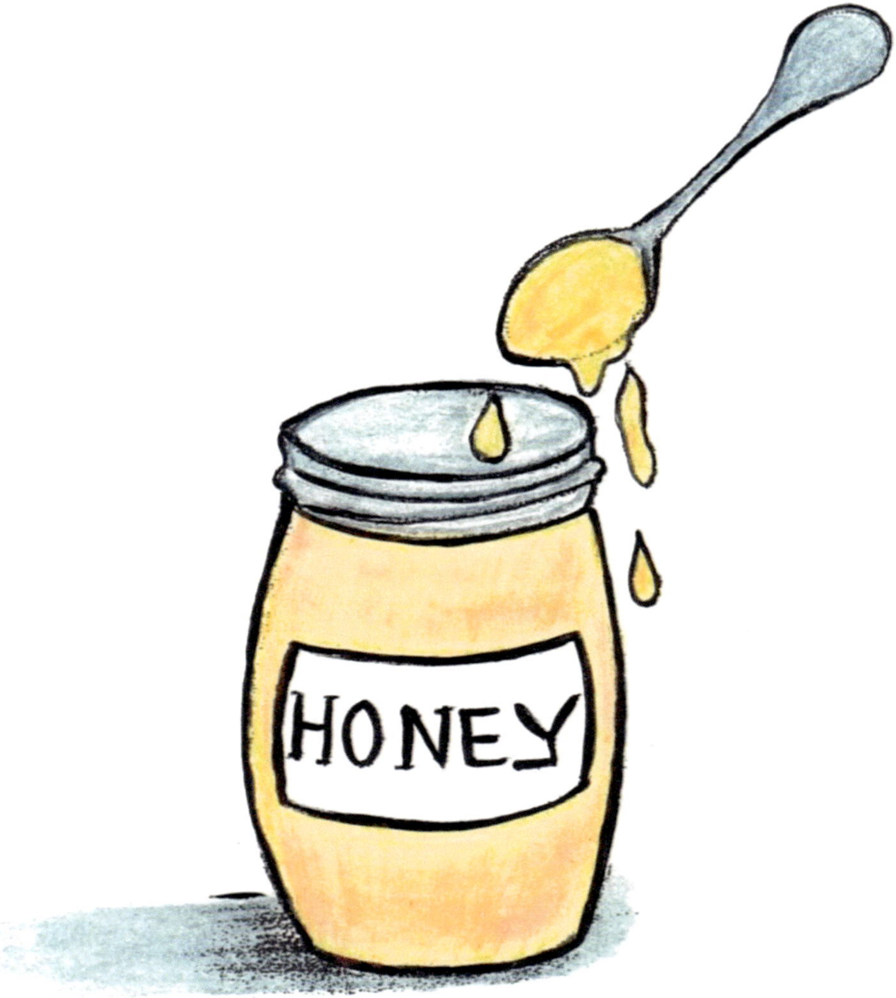
HONEY

But as I explain it, these bees and honey and stuff,

Puck-A-Gin, don't act real excited, like he don't listen enough.

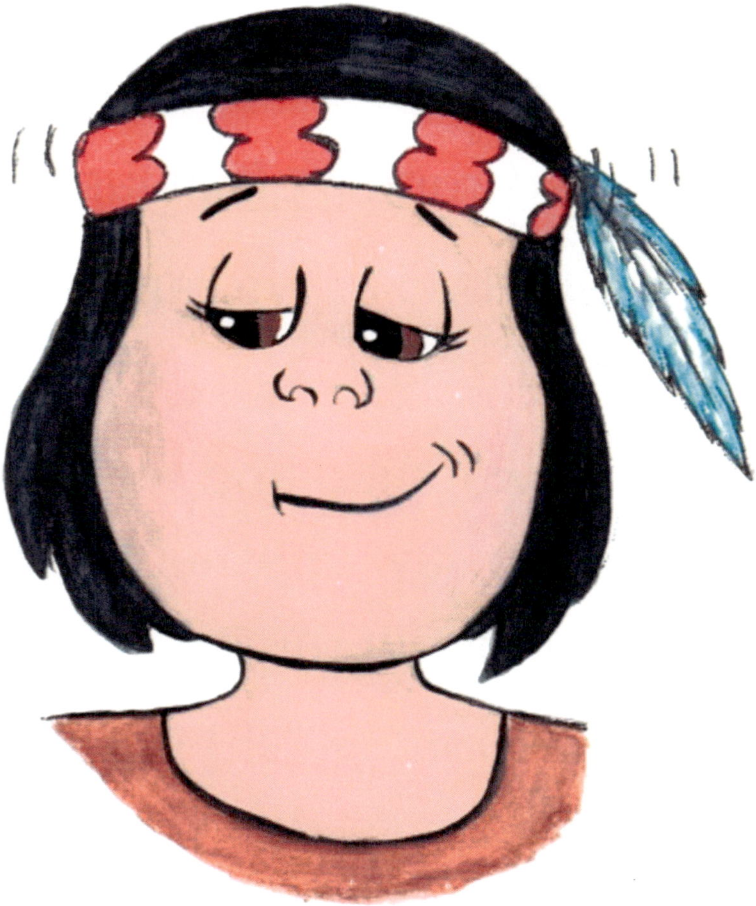

There's a bee!

Let's follow him!

We start running real fast!

We watched as we ran, but we lost him at last.

So, we watched and we waited and soon saw another, flying straight down the hill.

All this running, Oh! Brother!

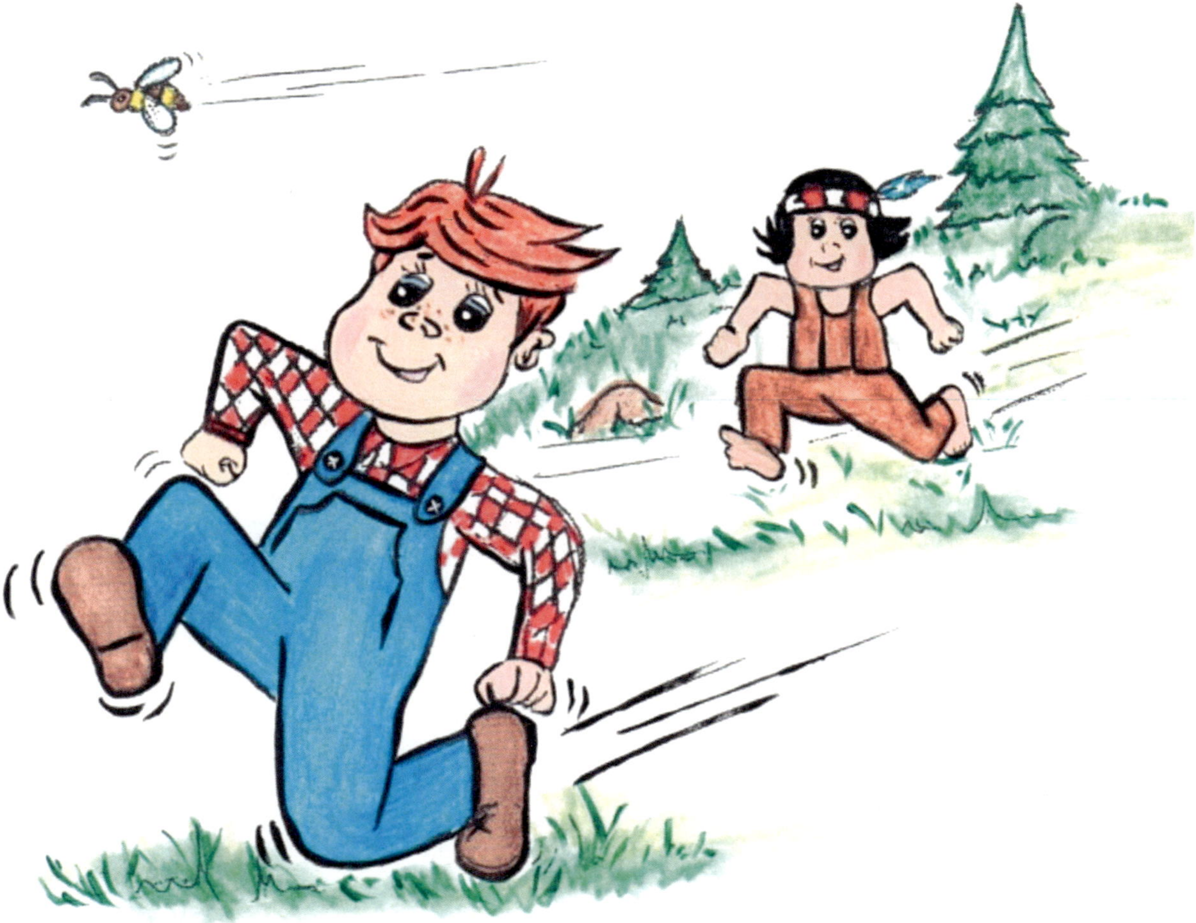

We ran stumbling and falling wound up like a nest.

When we finally stopped rolling I saw it at last.

There it was, up high in that old weathered tree.

If you watched it real close you could see many a bee.

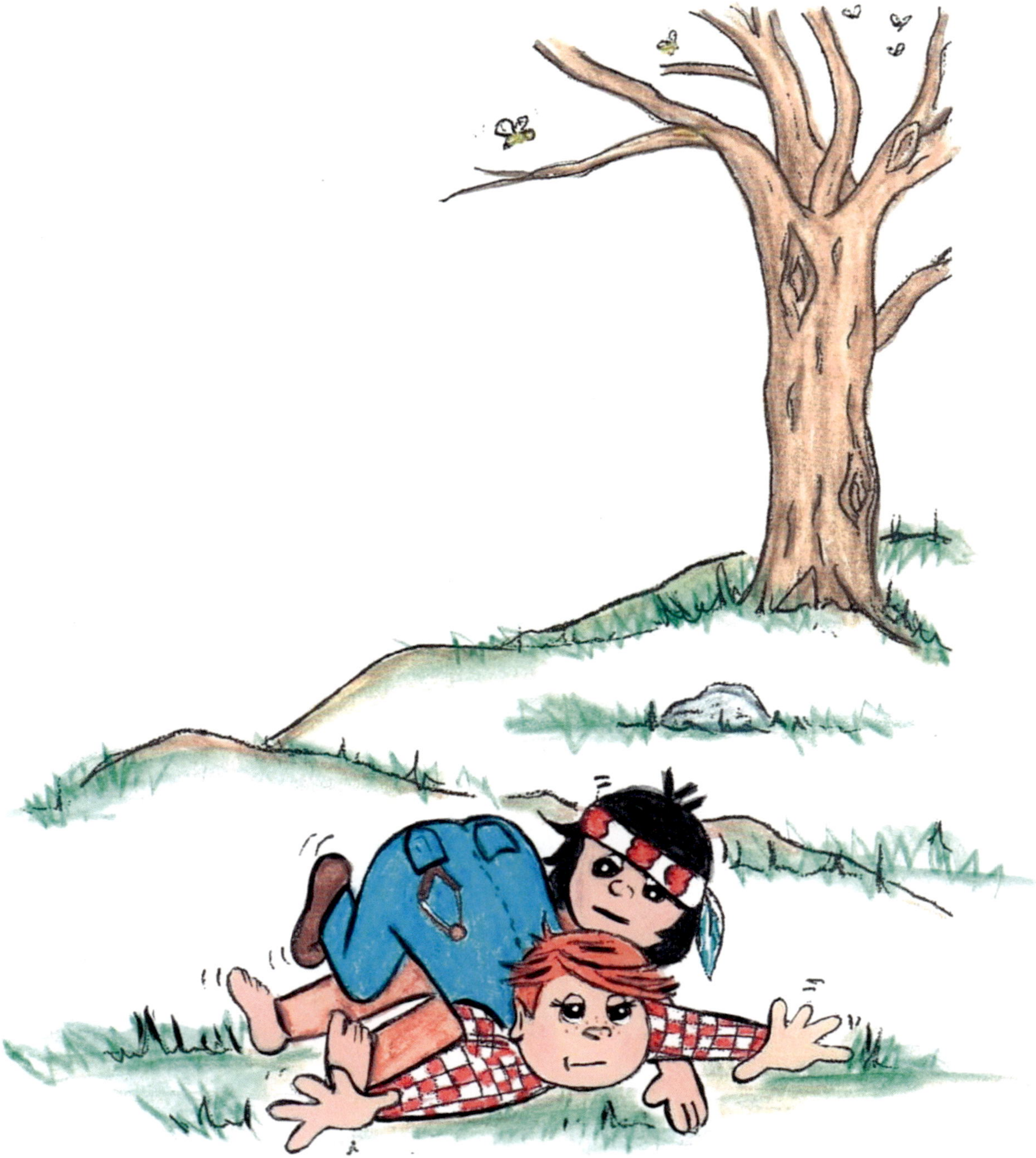

I said,"You know, Puck-A-Gin, what we need is some honey to eat."

As I pointed up there, he started shuffling his feet.

He took a few steps back, and started shaking his head.

Sometimes, I could never figure out all the things that he said.

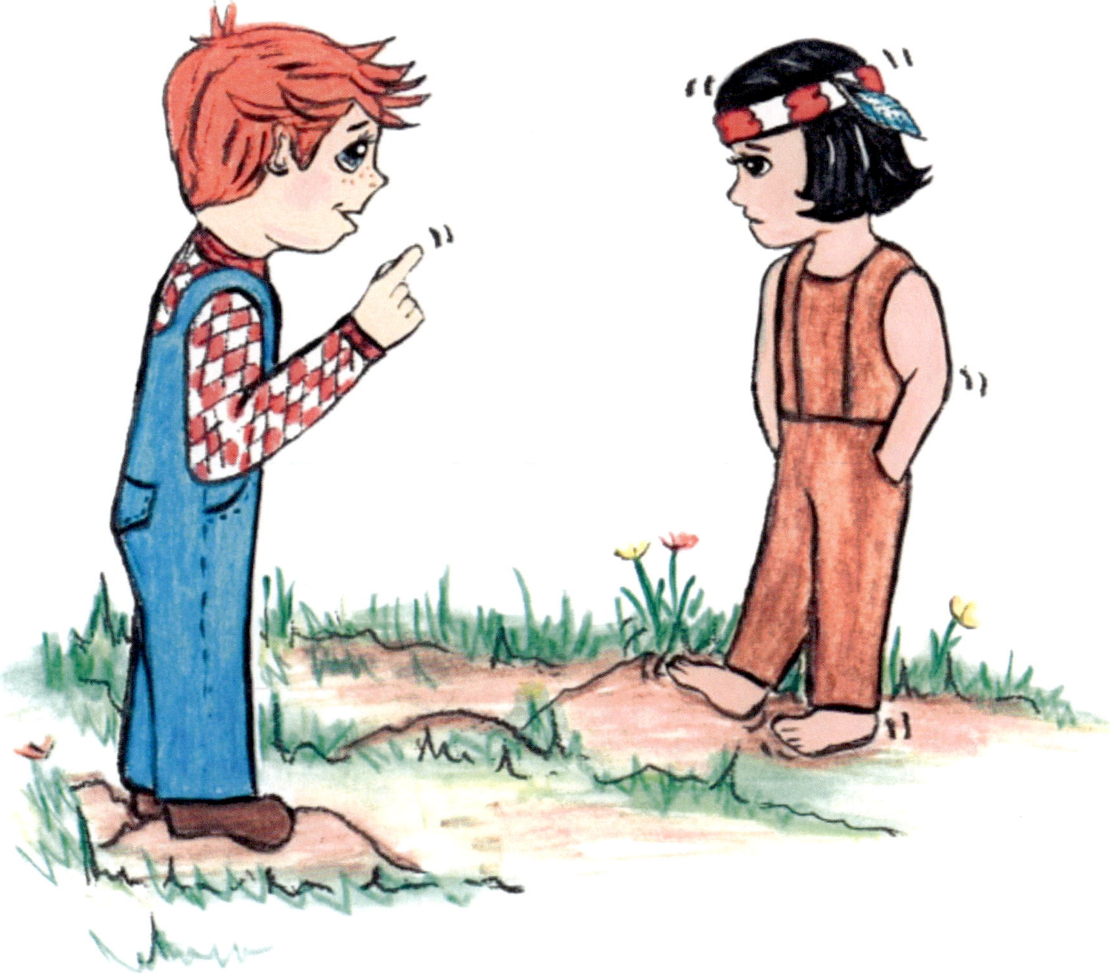

I started climbing the tree, for that sweet honey treat.

Soon I got real close, and that honey to eat.

But the bees had stopped flying

And started looking around.

Then like all at once, they came and knocked me to the ground.

One stung me on the arm, and three times on the head.

Now I just figured out what Puck-A-Gin said!

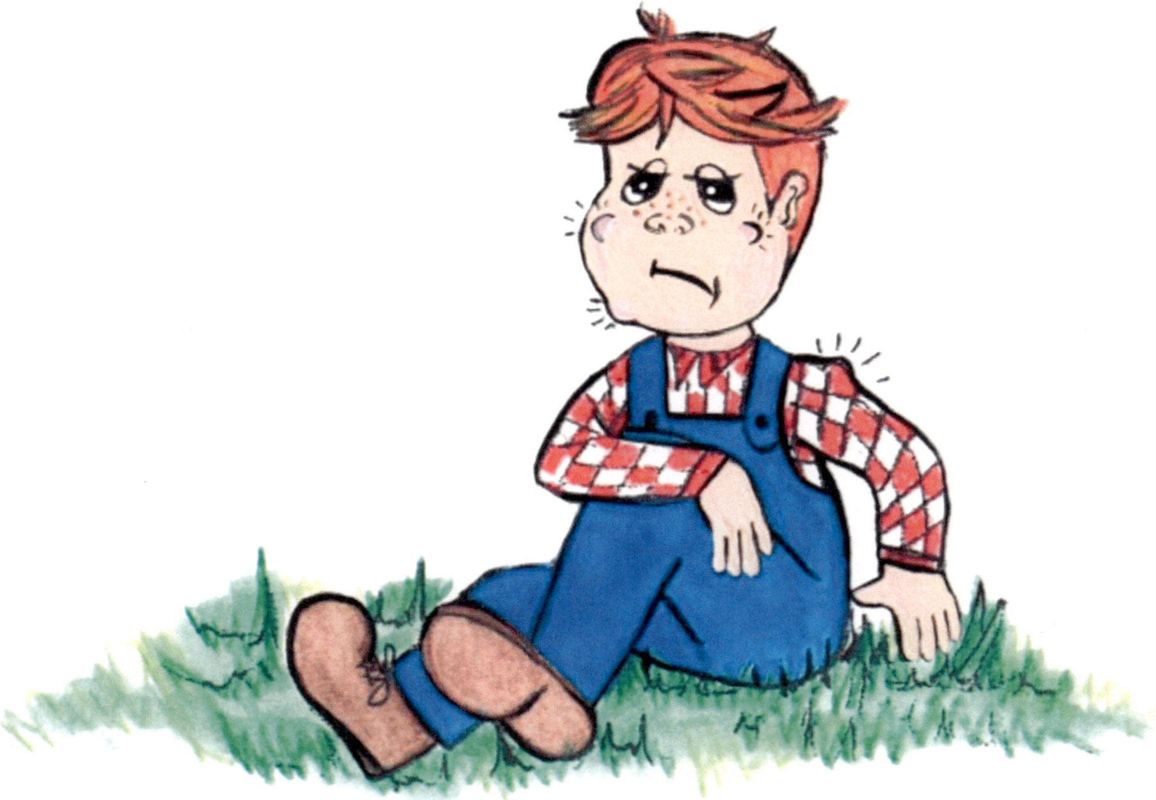

I rolled and I tossed around on the ground!

And jumped up and ran, til no bees were found!

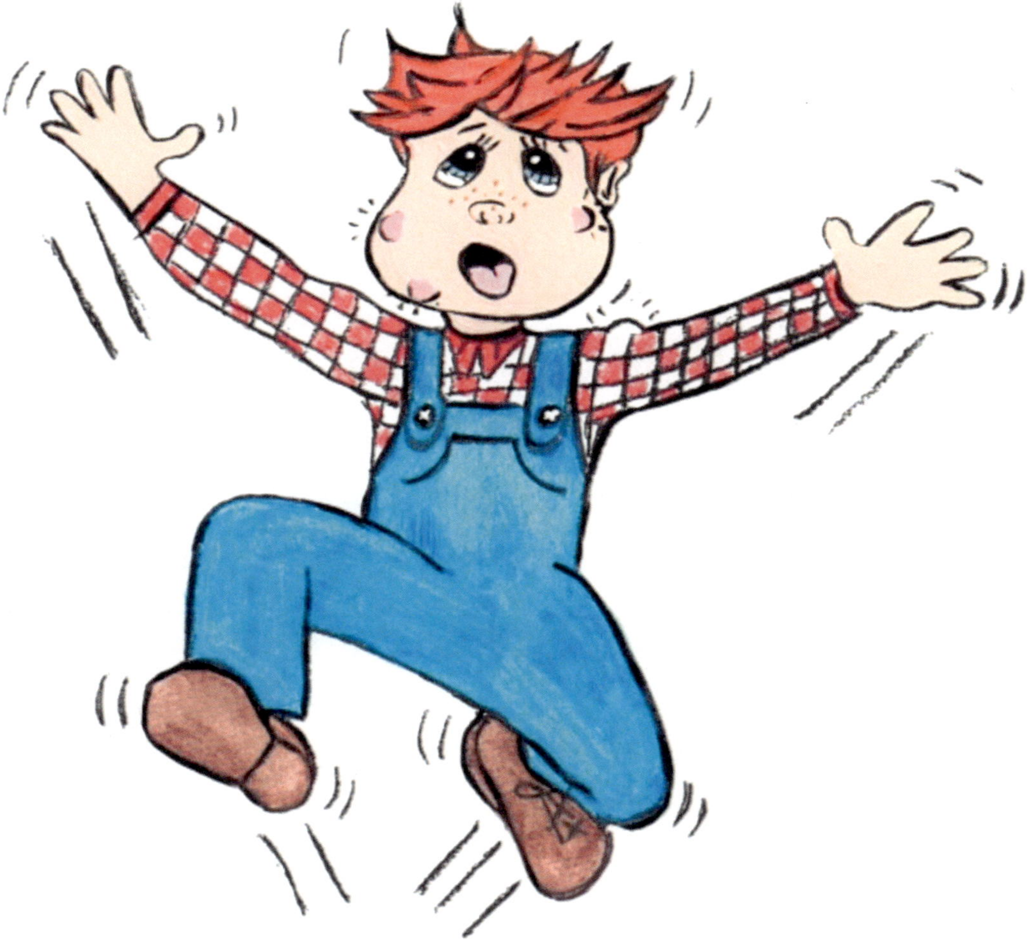

Puck-A-Gin rolled and he laughed, when he saw me alright.

I guess I was really jumping, from all those busy bee bites!

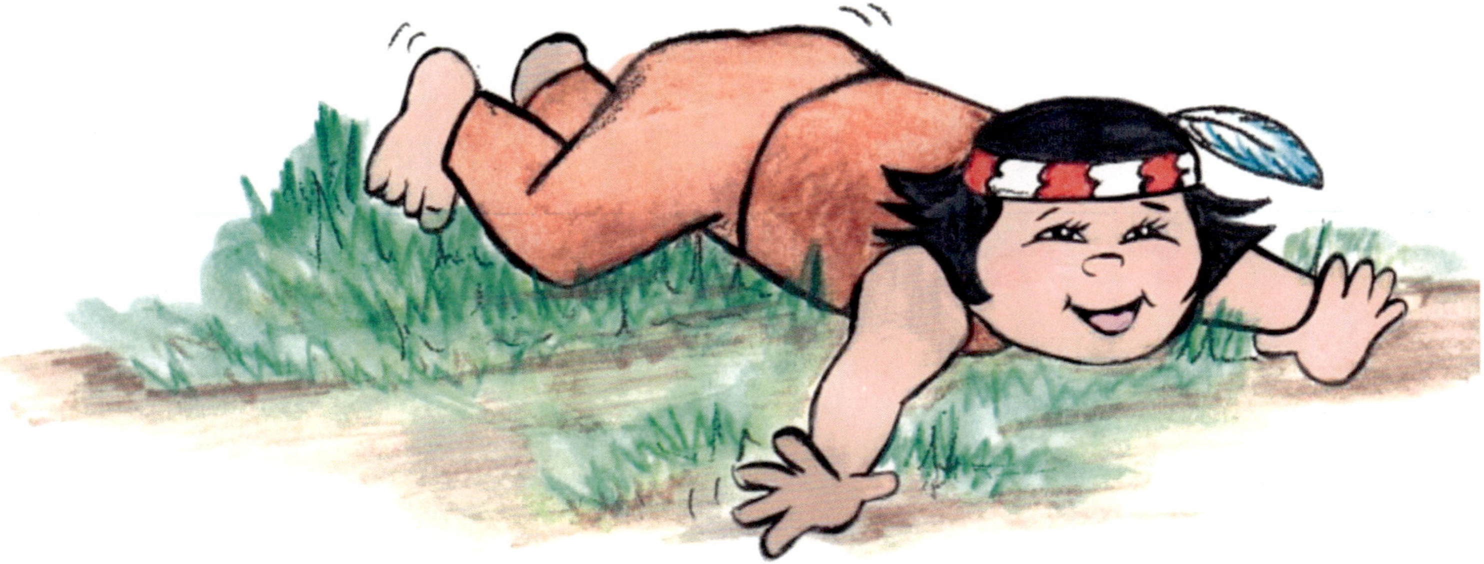

Then Puck-A-Gin took me down
by the clear water pool.

And gathered mud dobbs to put
on the bites, that felt kind of cool.

He motioned at me, and then
laughed over and over again.

I finally had to laugh too, with

my friend Puck-A-Gin.

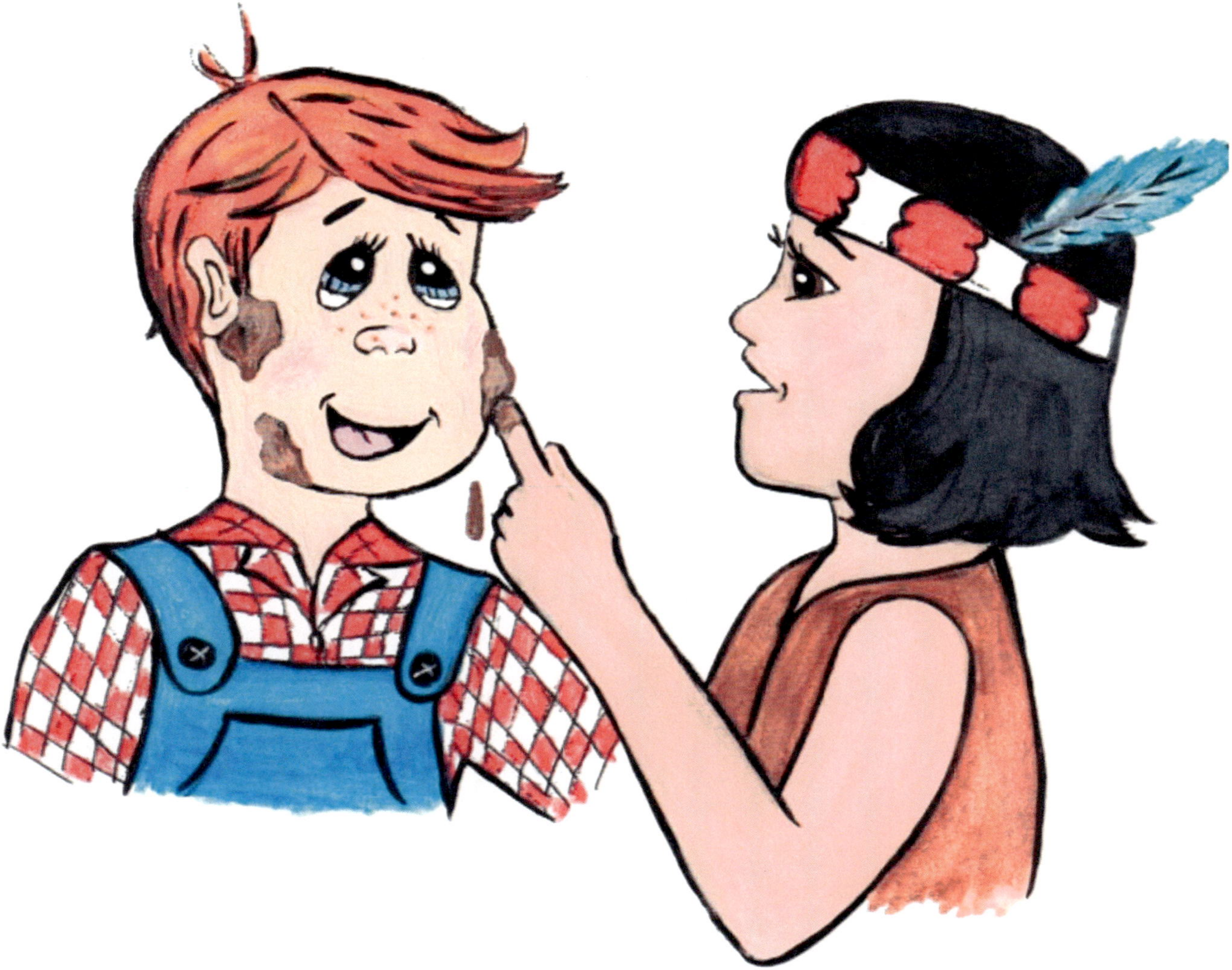

You know sometimes plans don't work out as we think they should.

And next time, I'd better listen, and listen, real good!

Now with the swelling and all I must look quite a sight!

I guess once is enough, to be

"A Mud Dobber's Delight."

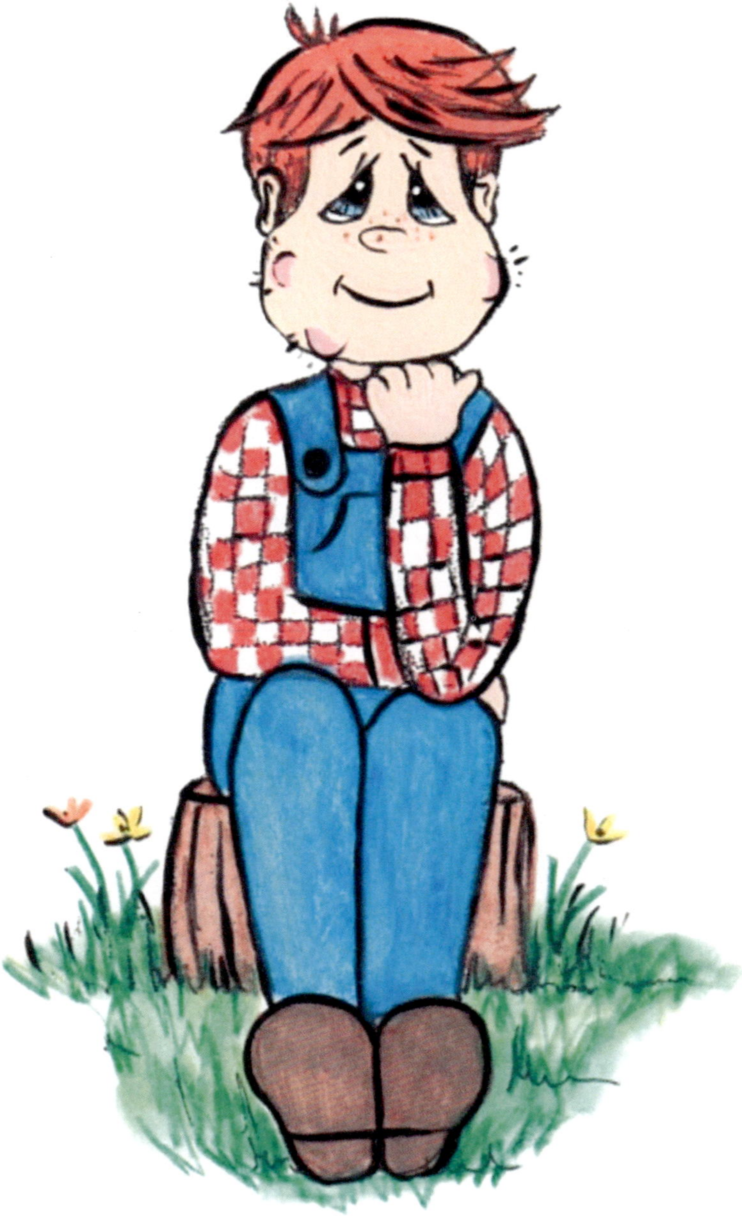

The End

74

Mildred the Moo

Story by **Larry L. Maxwell**

Artwork by **Frankie A. Maxwell**

Now mornings soon came, as all mornings do,

With Rastus now crowing and Mildred The Moo.

Now Mildred was most gentle, a gentle milk cow,

As she chewed on her tongue trying to eat it somehow.

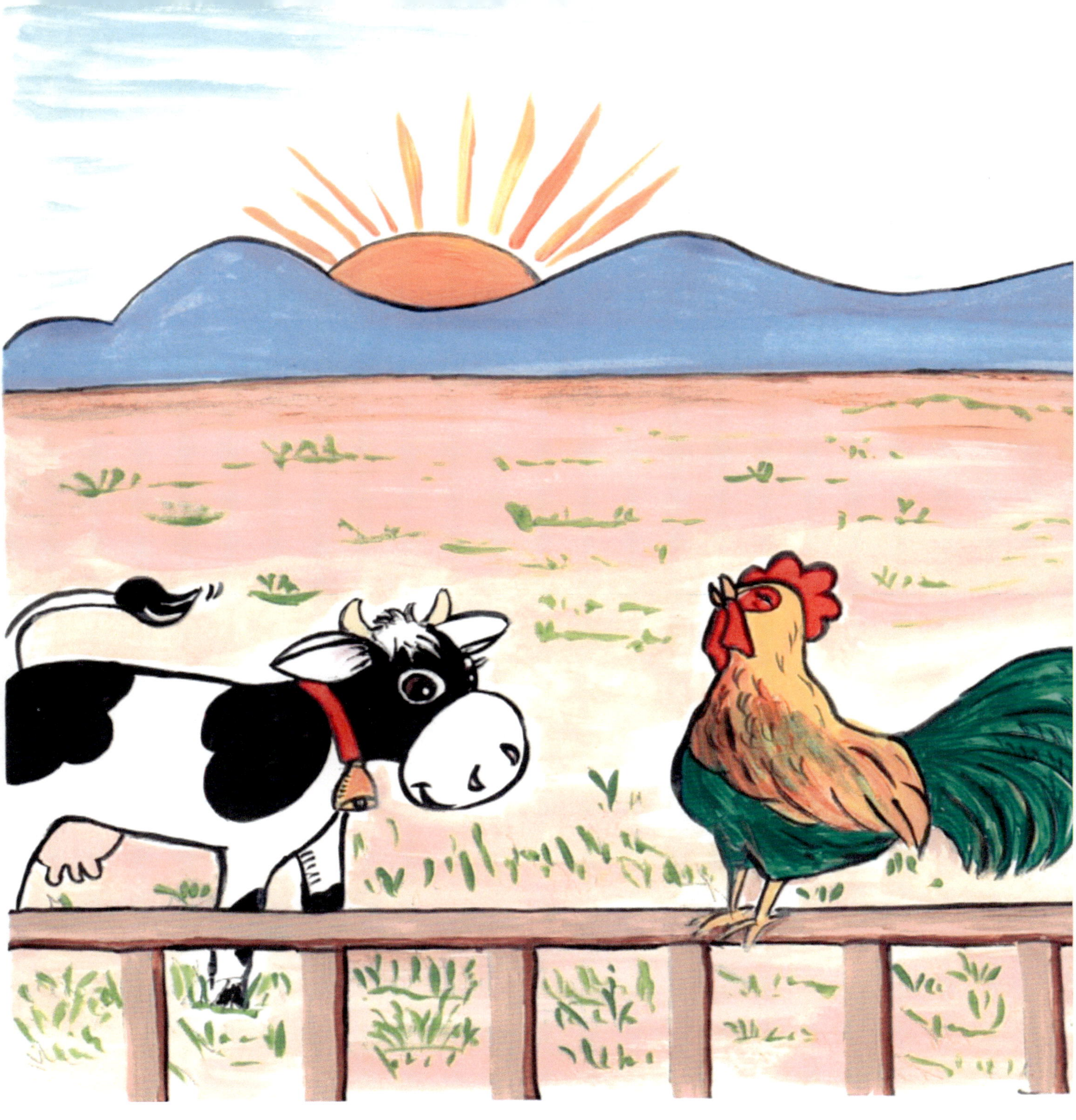

I have watched her do that even before the hay.

Dad says there's that Mildred, just chewing away.

I've looked in her mouth, as I petted her hair,

And to my surprise there was no food in there.

Now I've watched her a lot, I really wanted to know

Why Mildred the milk cow would always chew so.

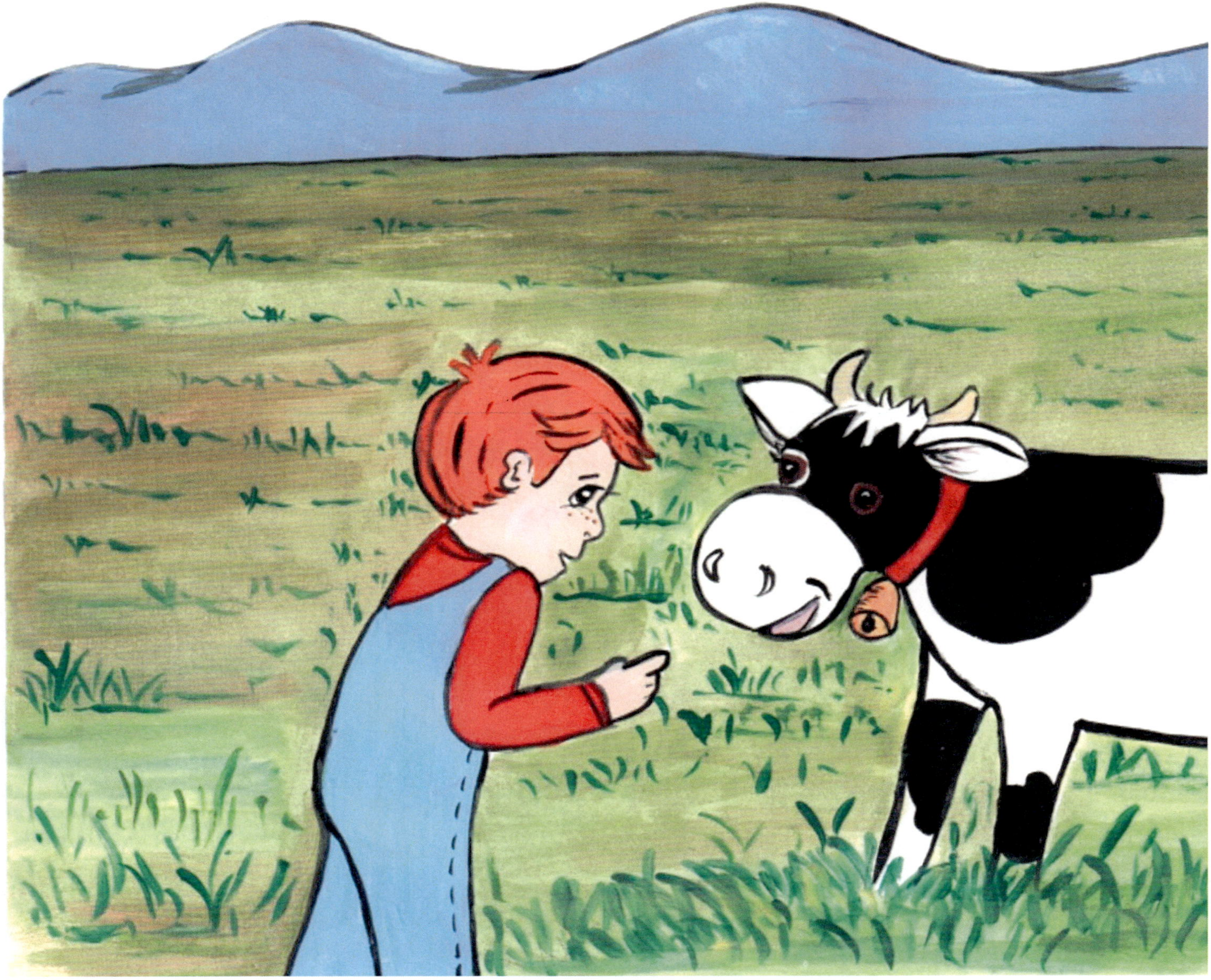

It was this same Mildred that we tracked right in. It was on that scouting trip, me and Puck-A-Gin.

Dad milks her each morning, or so it may seem. He gets buckets of white milk, and Mildred's great cream

I guess my job is to watch her all night and all day. Cause dad always says it's work before play.

Now to me and my side kick, this seems kind of rough. It's time always wasted from our real special stuff.

Sometimes I keep watch in those great summer days.

It's down near the cornfield, that she likes to graze.

She's gone! Where did she go?

That Mildred The Moo?

There she is in the corn, Oh! Boy!

Now what do I do?

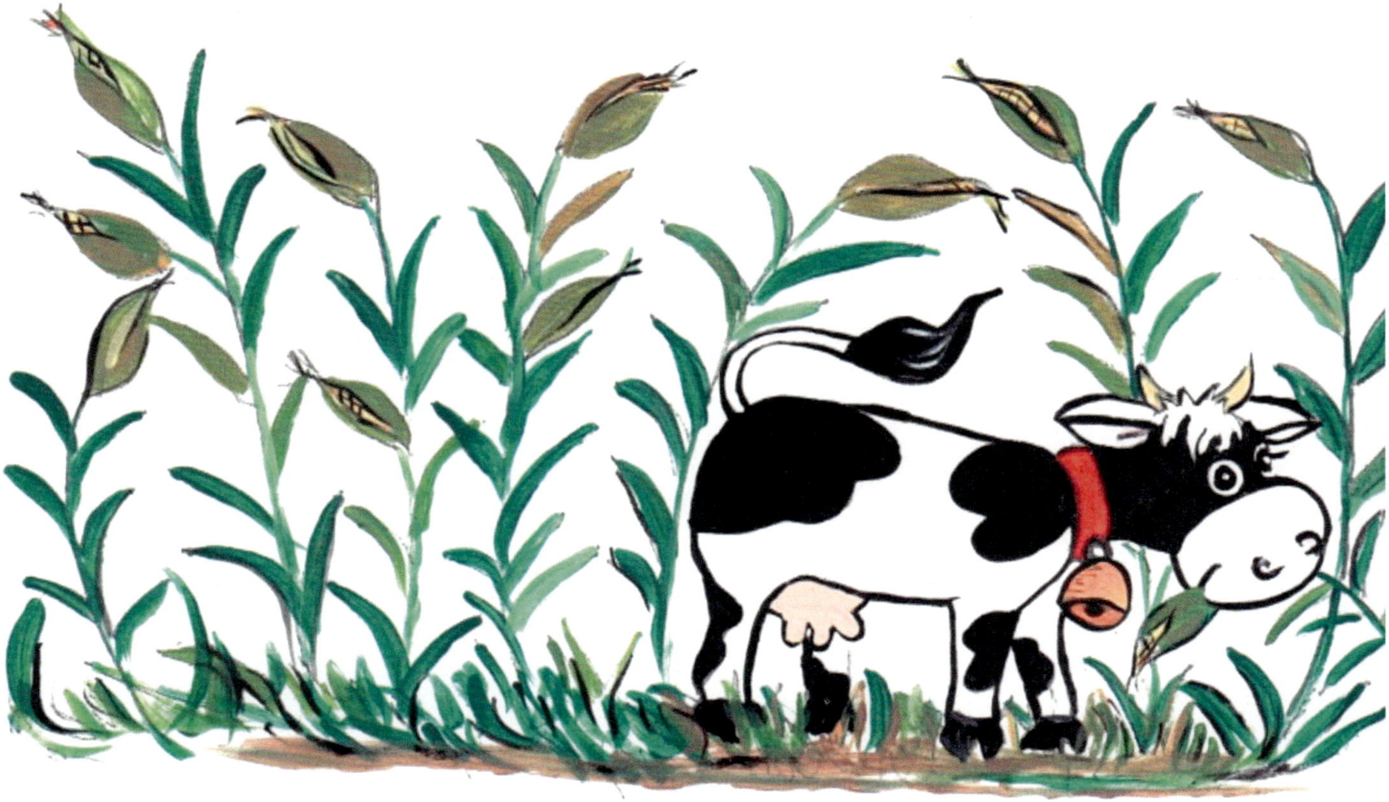

Now get out of there!

Get along there!

Now shoo!

You big sassy cow - that Mildred The Moo.

Boy! Will I ever be glad when this day is done.

It's a heck of a job, for Dad's favorite son.

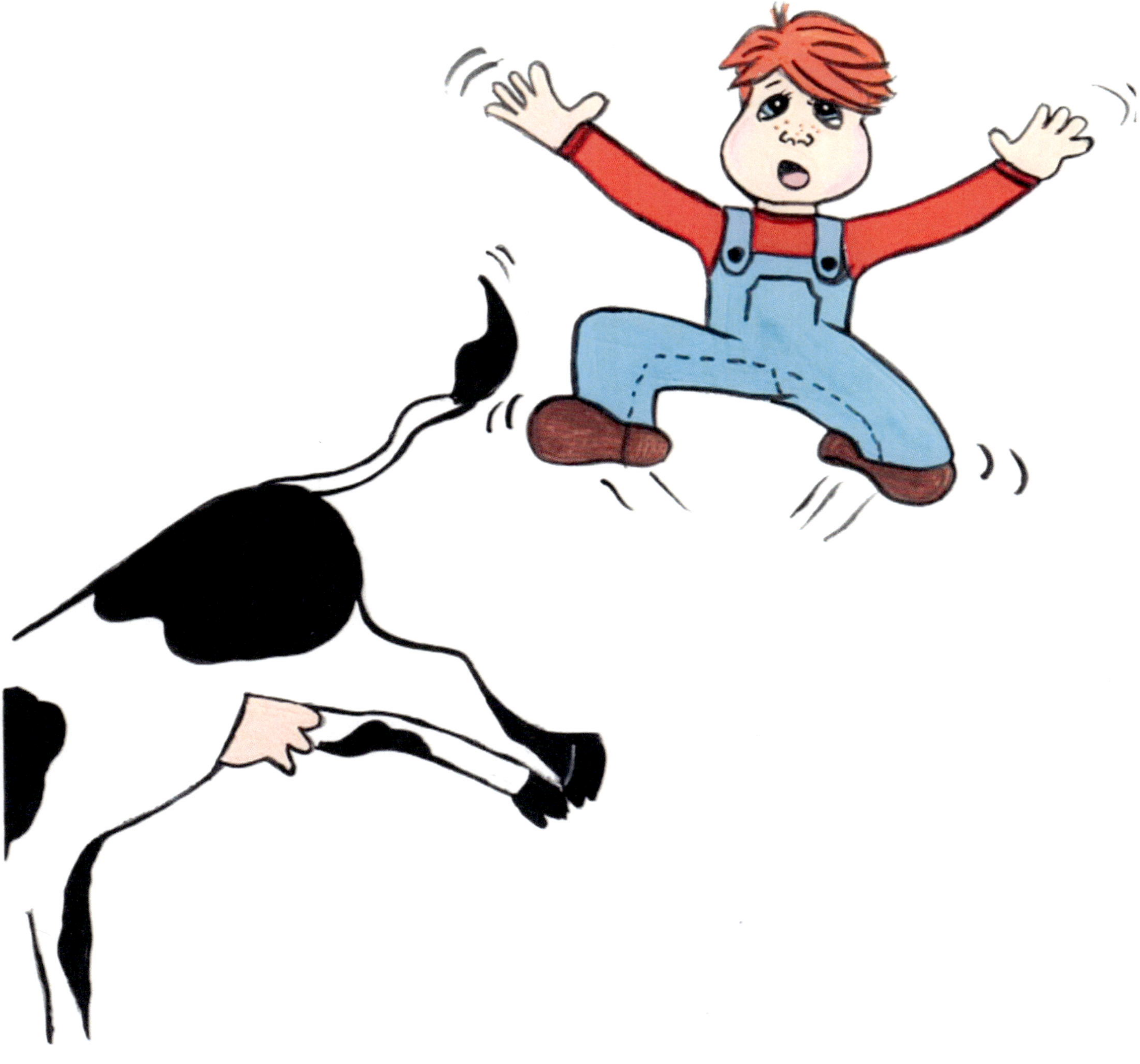

Maybe I should be an Indian, like my Indian friend.

He don't have this trouble with cows,

My friend Puck -A-Gin.

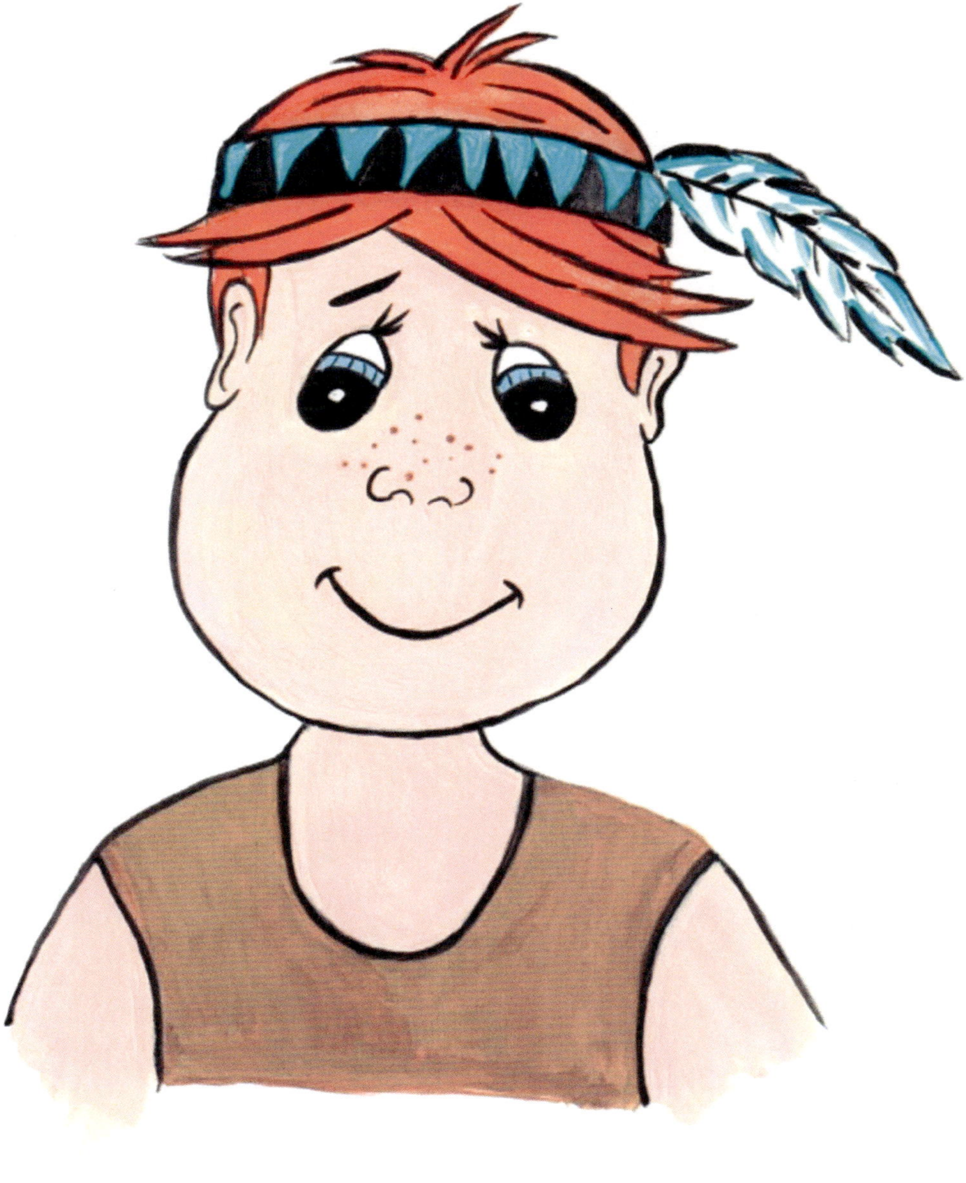

But I guess it's a job, like all farm boys do.

I guess it isn't so bad to watch Mildred The Moo.

Besides Dad's home – Mom yells, "Suppers Ready!"

And Dad tells Mom out loud, like he's especially proud,

"My Smitty"

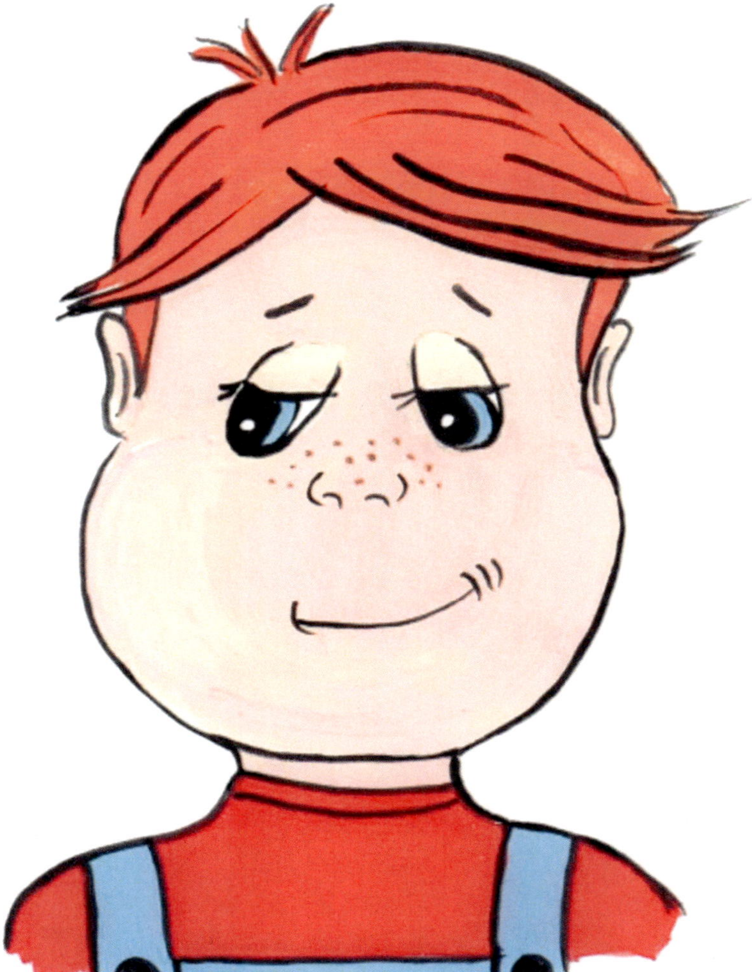

The End

Arrow of Stone

Story by **Larry L. Maxwell**

Artwork by **Frankie A. Maxwell**

The early crisp of morning fresh air.

Reminded Puck-A-Gin of his leaving that was already there.

His dad said the sheep must move to the valley below.

Away from the cold and winter's deep snow.

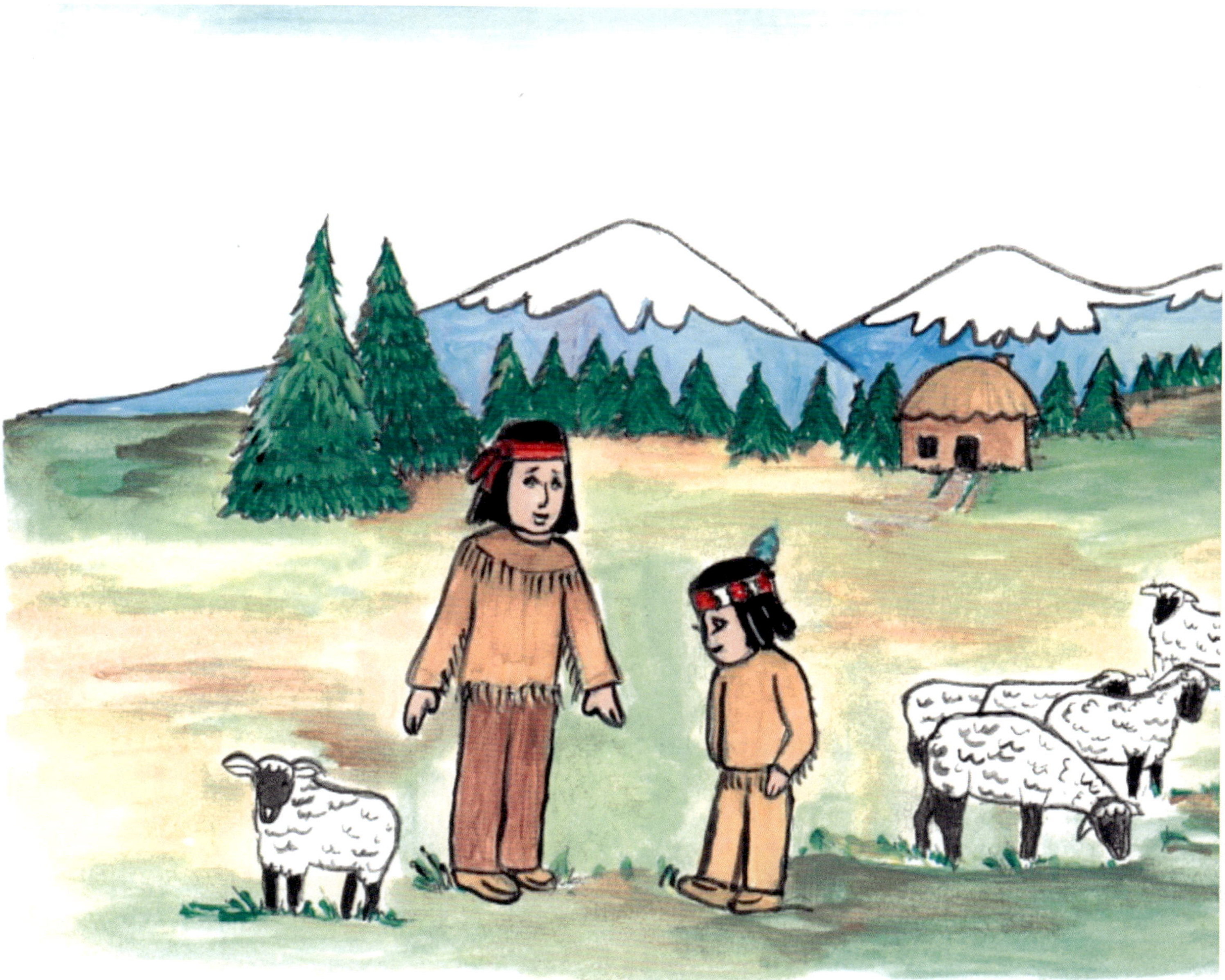

All were up early, and pushing downhill real strong.

Puck-A-Gin went with the rest but was kinda dragging along.

He knew he would be leaving,

And would never be ready.

And how tell his friend, the fire haired Mitty?

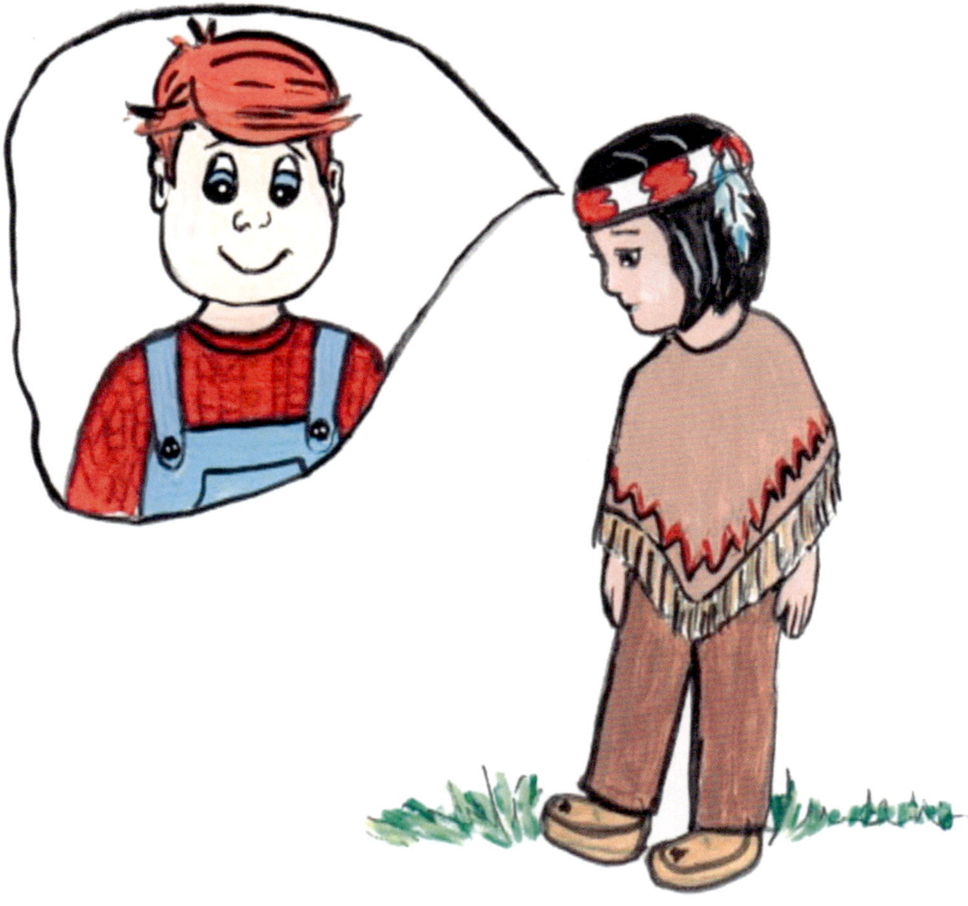

They had the greatest of times, and just so much to do.

And where he was going, there was everything new.

He walked to the ledge and looked toward Smitty asleep in his bed.

And thought maybe it's better this way,

These things left unsaid.

He'd leave him a way – An arrow –
A sign.

Made of round river rocks, that Smitty would find.

And his favorite bow, and his arrows too.

Now with a tear on his cheek – He'd know Smitty knew.

For sometimes there are friends that go on forever.

And he thought of his Mitty and the bend in the river.

Then all the good things came racing along.

It's nice thought Puck-A-Gin when you really belong.

He thought maybe sometime – Someday, "I will see this Mitty."

As he moved through the light and saw his dad standing ready.

He motioned to Puck-A-Gin, to move them in tight. They moved down the hill in the fresh morning light.

The cool morning found little Smitty up bright.

He felt kind of strange, from his restless sleep night.

A walk in the woods would help out and see Puck-A-Gin's face,

Would calm any doubt and help problems erase.

He didn't quite know, why he just felt kind of bad.

It wasn't usually the way of Smitty the lad.

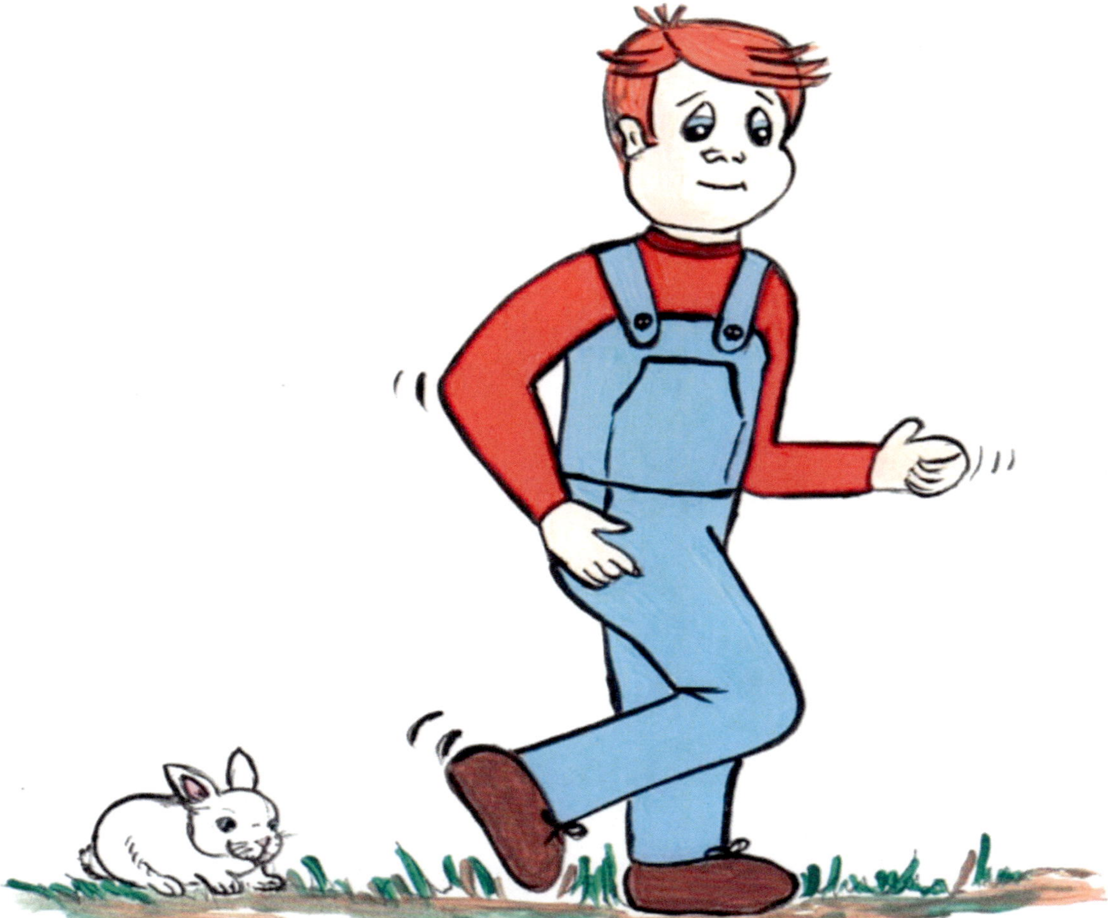

Yet there it was, something for sure over and over again.

Oh well! It would be fine when he saw Puck-A-Gin.

And then there he saw it – The arrow of stone.

The carefully laid bow, he knew Puck-A-Gin was gone.

He finally went home, feeling sad and alone.

As he held arrow and bow, and thought of the arrow of stone.

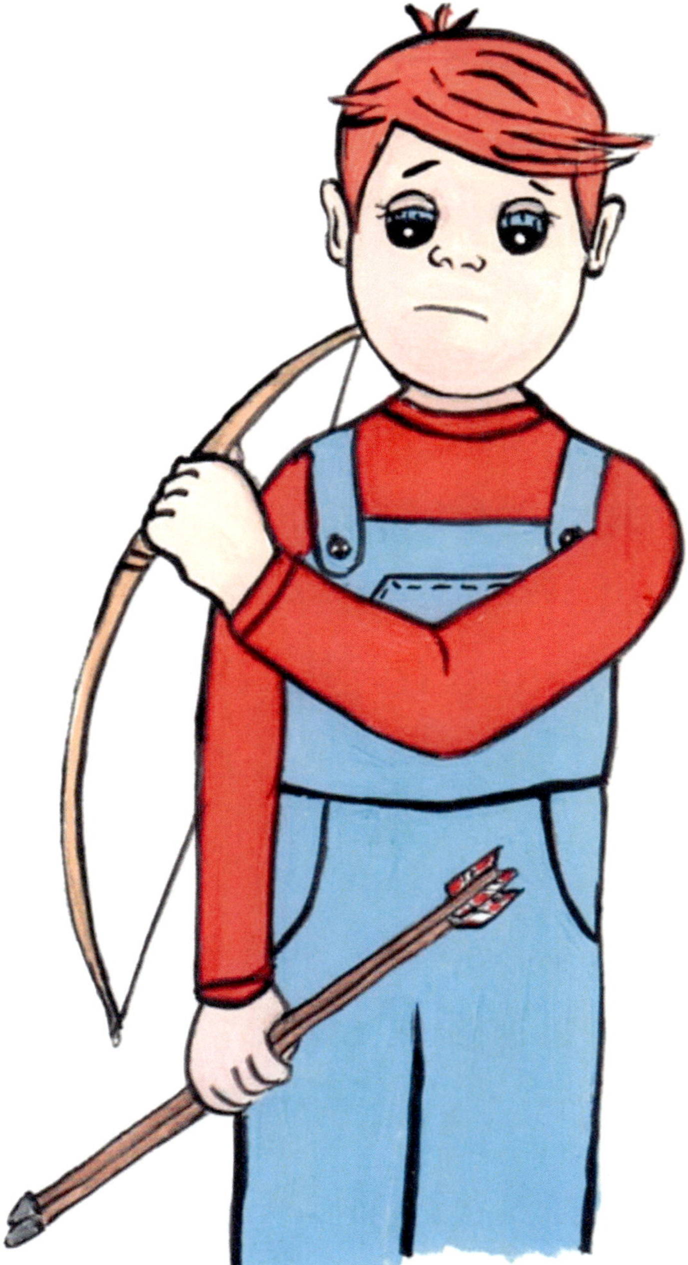

Then dad came by and rubbed my ruffled red head.

I guess he already knew what my friend Puck-A-Gin did.

So he sat by my side and said, "Smitty, you know Puck-A-Gin needed to leave sometime before snow. And I know he is special, but needed to go. Don't be so sad, let me tell you a thing, now take it from dad."

"You may one day see each other, sometime once again, so remember the good times, about you and Puck-A-Gin."

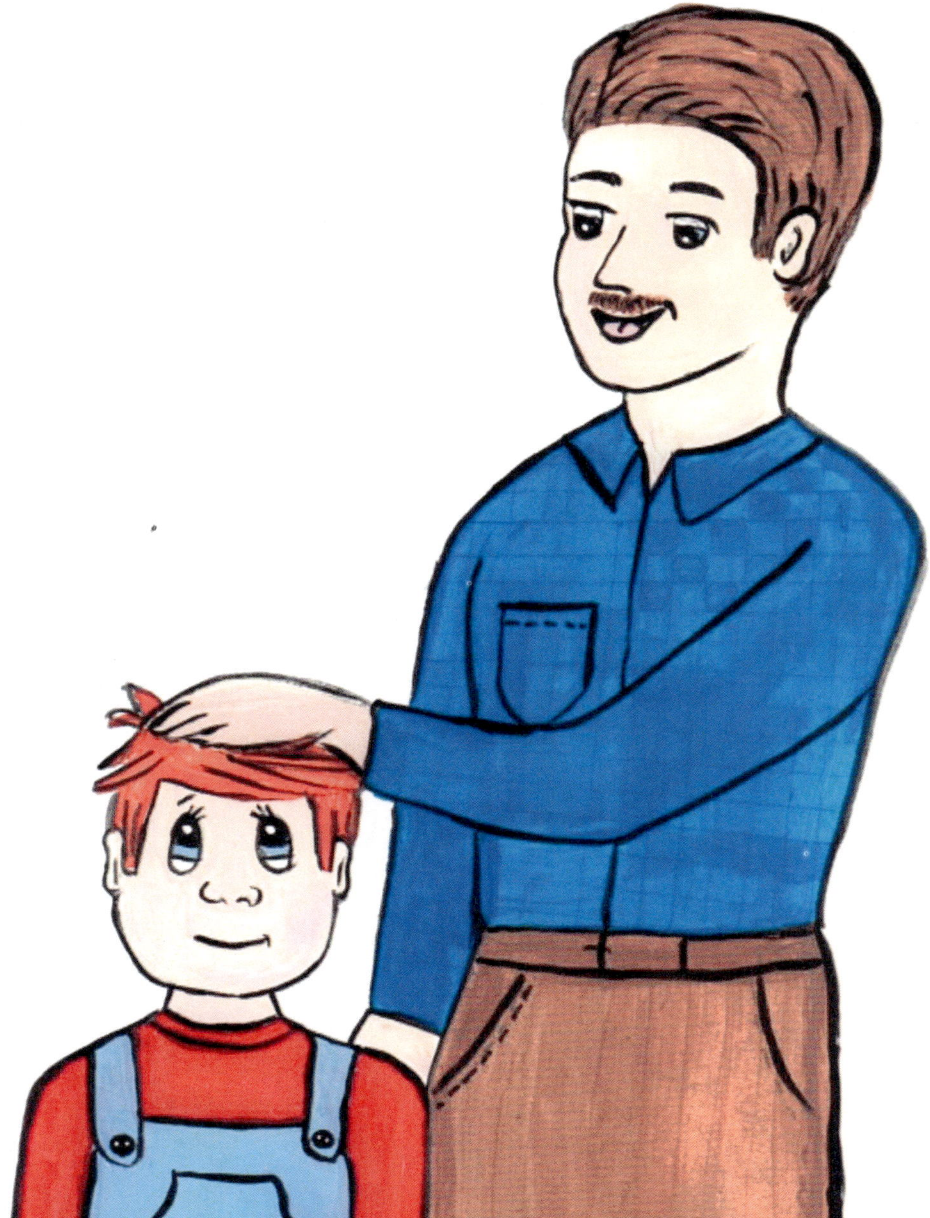

Sometimes things aren't easy, and sometimes a little sad.

But he will always be special, and we love you my lad.

I've thought this all over and tried to be big already.

And I couldn't help smile to think how Puck-A-Gin said, "Mitty."

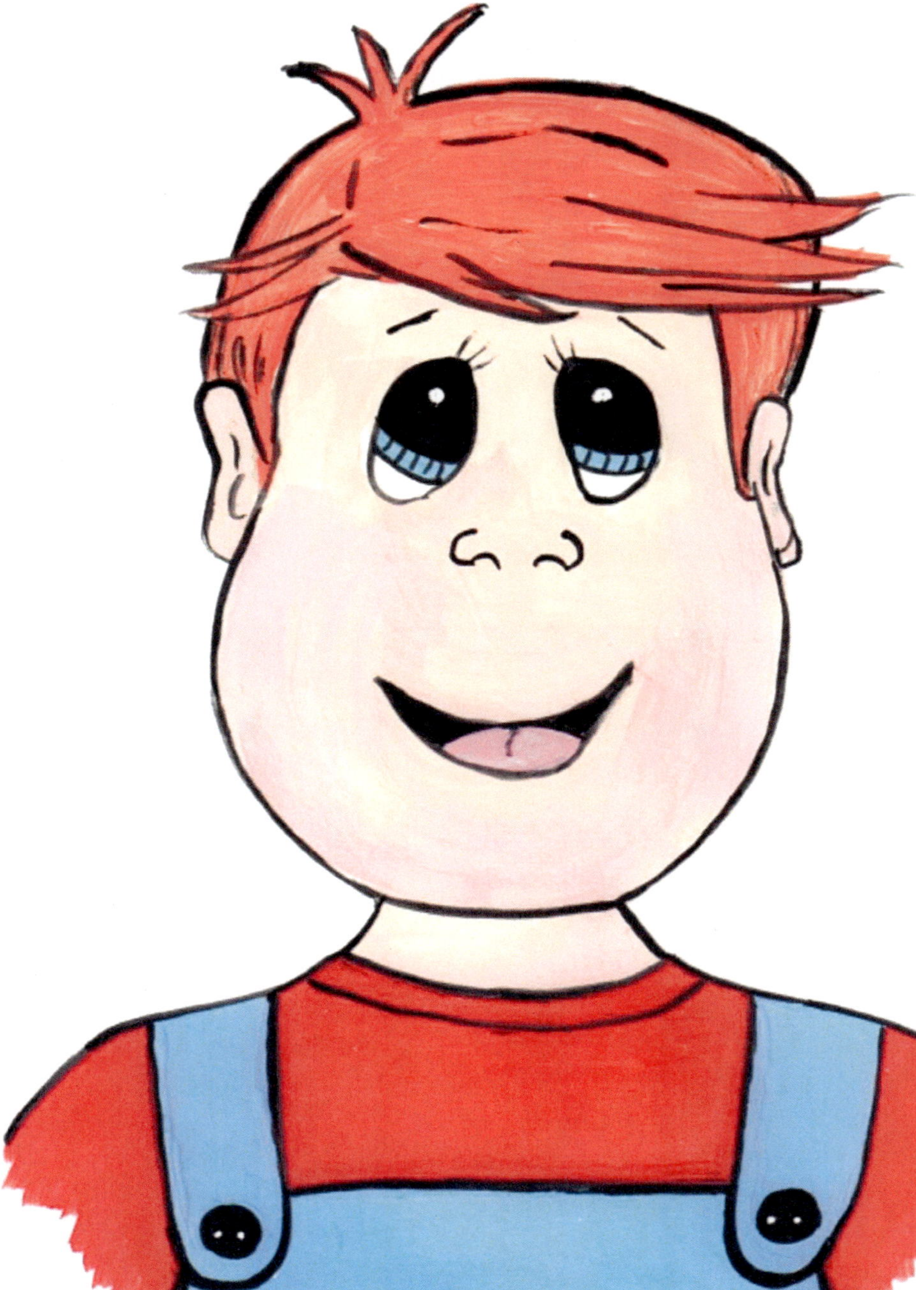

The End

Wampus Kitty

Story by Larry L. Maxwell

Artwork by Frankie A. Maxwell

Now little Smitty was quite a lad.

He was the best son his dad ever had.

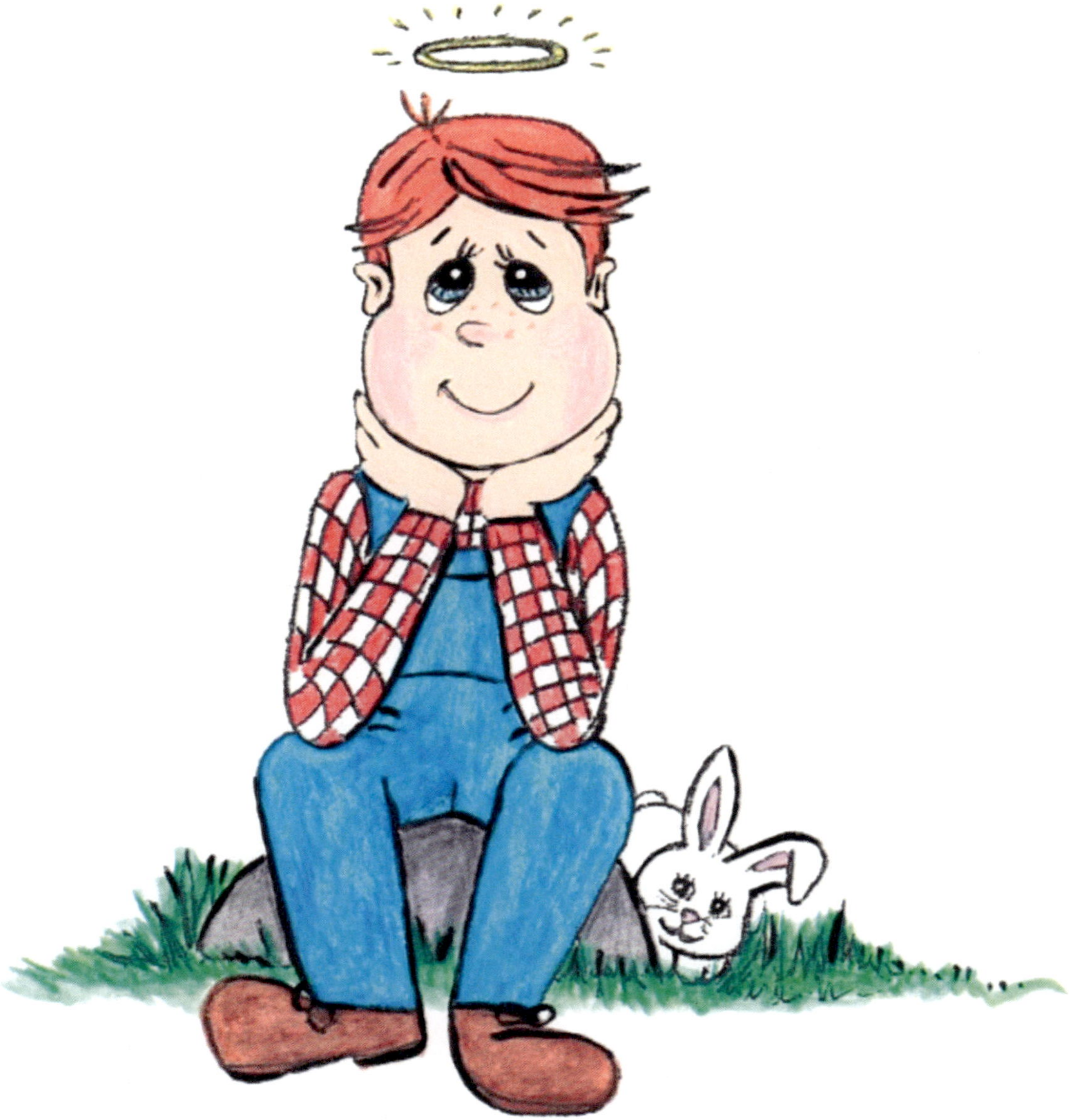

Come to think of it,

He was the only one.

His folks didn't have any other son.

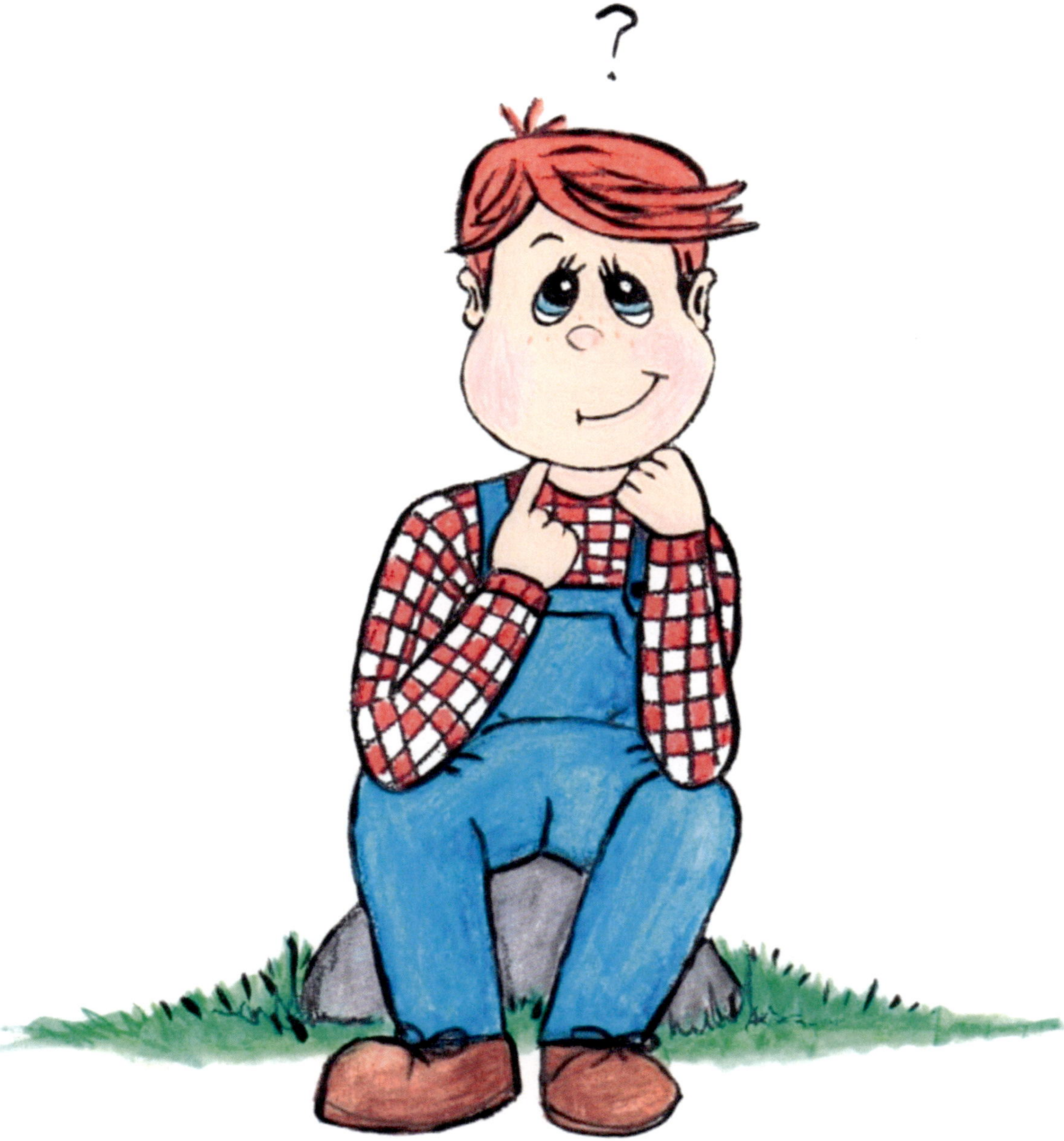

Even his hair flopped and his turned up nose

Was a special event right down to his toes.

His feet pointed out, or maybe a bit in.

He had a big smile, or was it a grin?

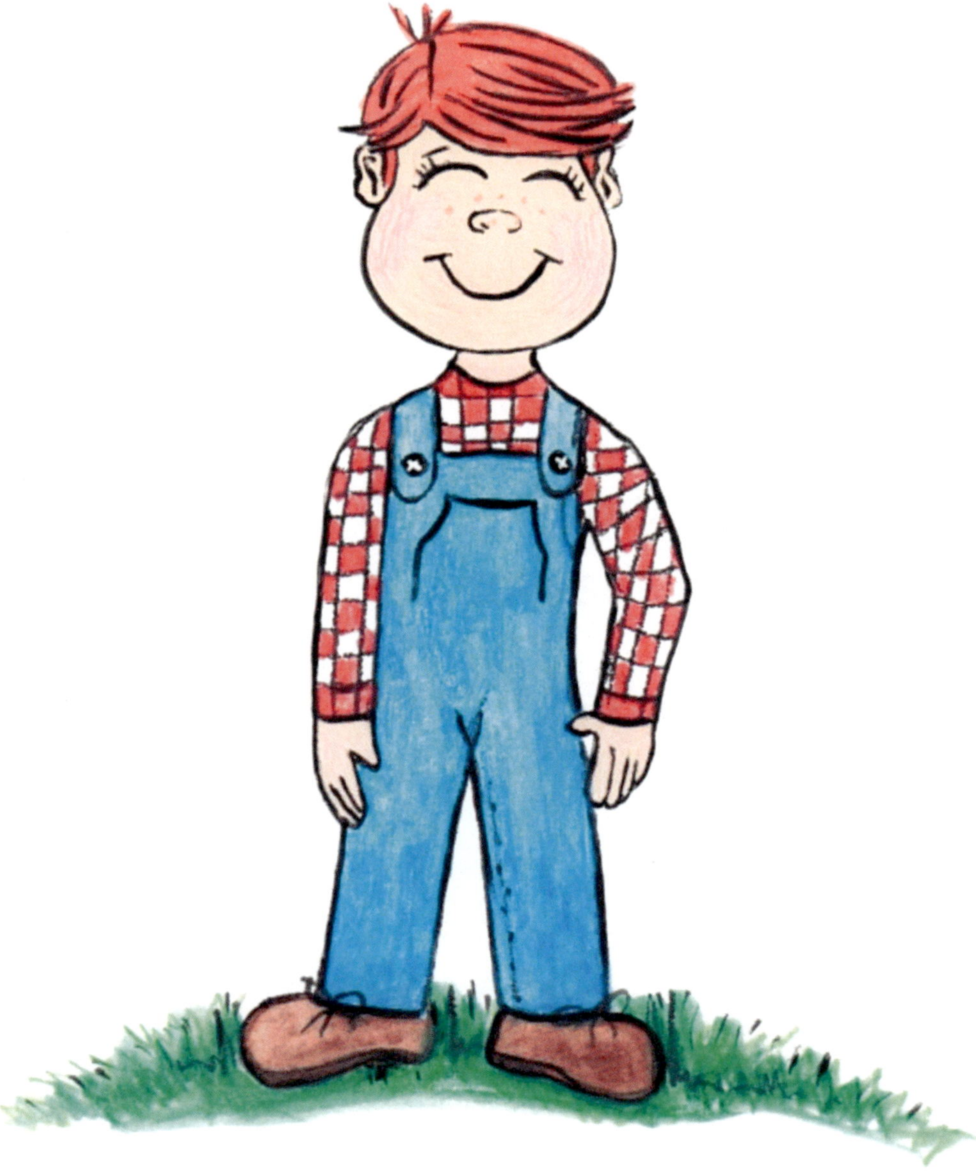

But sometimes, when it got time to be thinking

With big blue eyes, just blinking and blinking.

He watched other kids with their things and their pets,

Some even had dogs and others had cats.

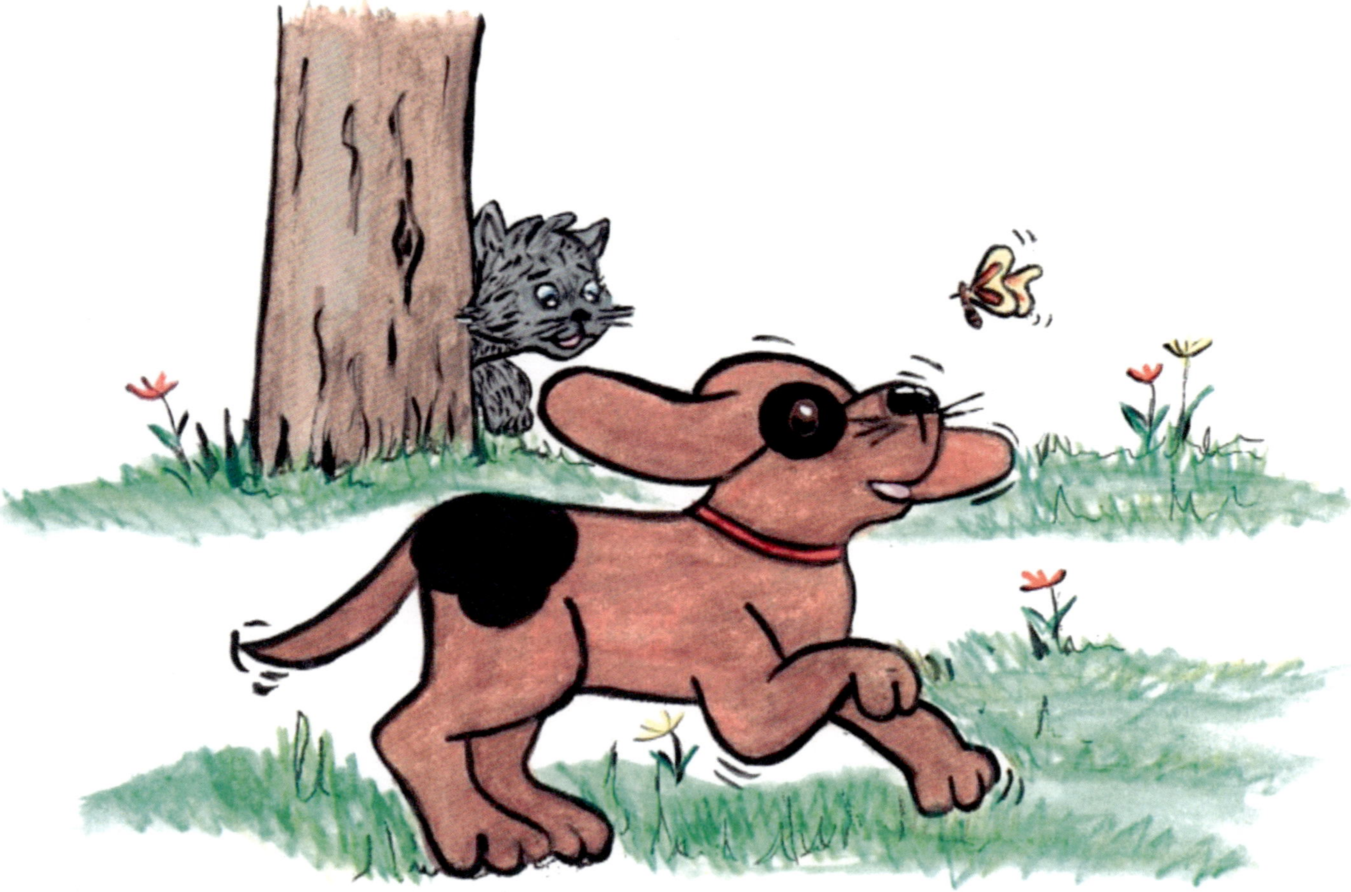

Then one day, Dad said,"Come along little Smitty."

"You're old enough now for your own little kitty."

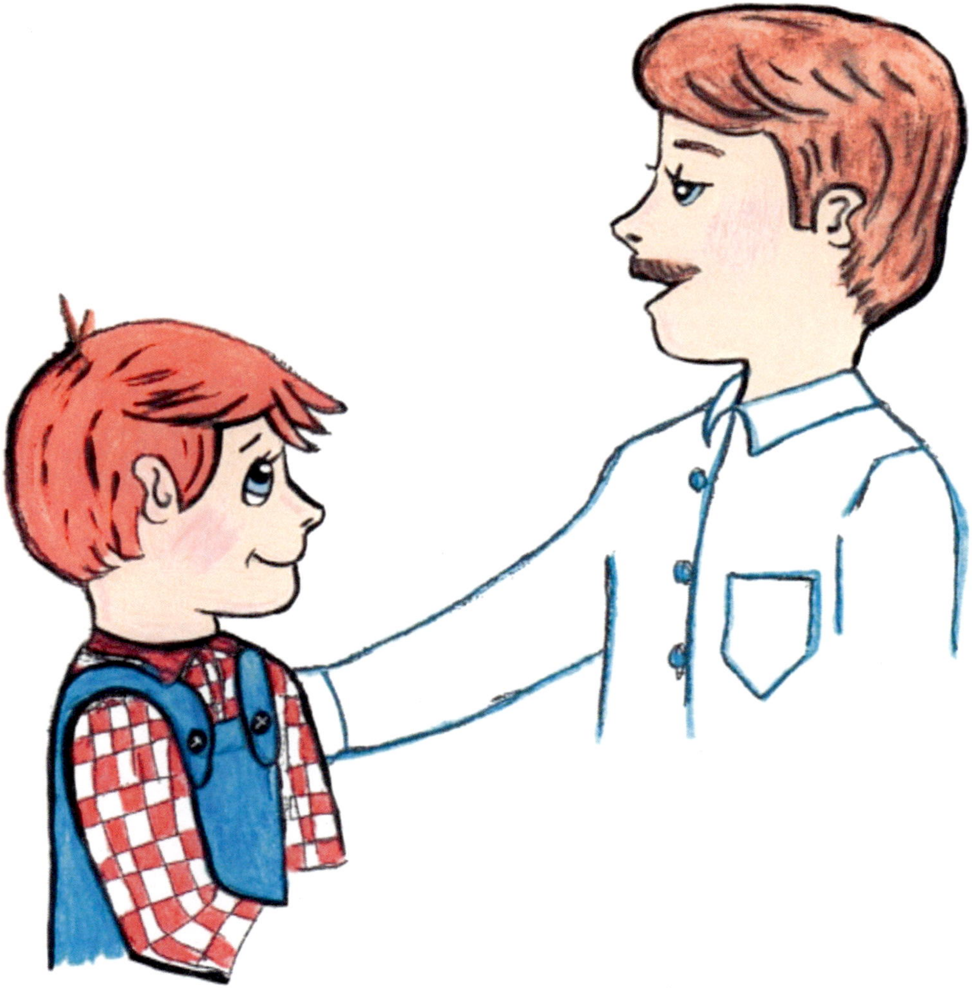

We searched the town over,

The farm yards the best

And when we had finished

We found one at last.

Now he wasn't to tall, or to short,

Or to pretty.

But Dad now assured me it was a Wampus Kitty.

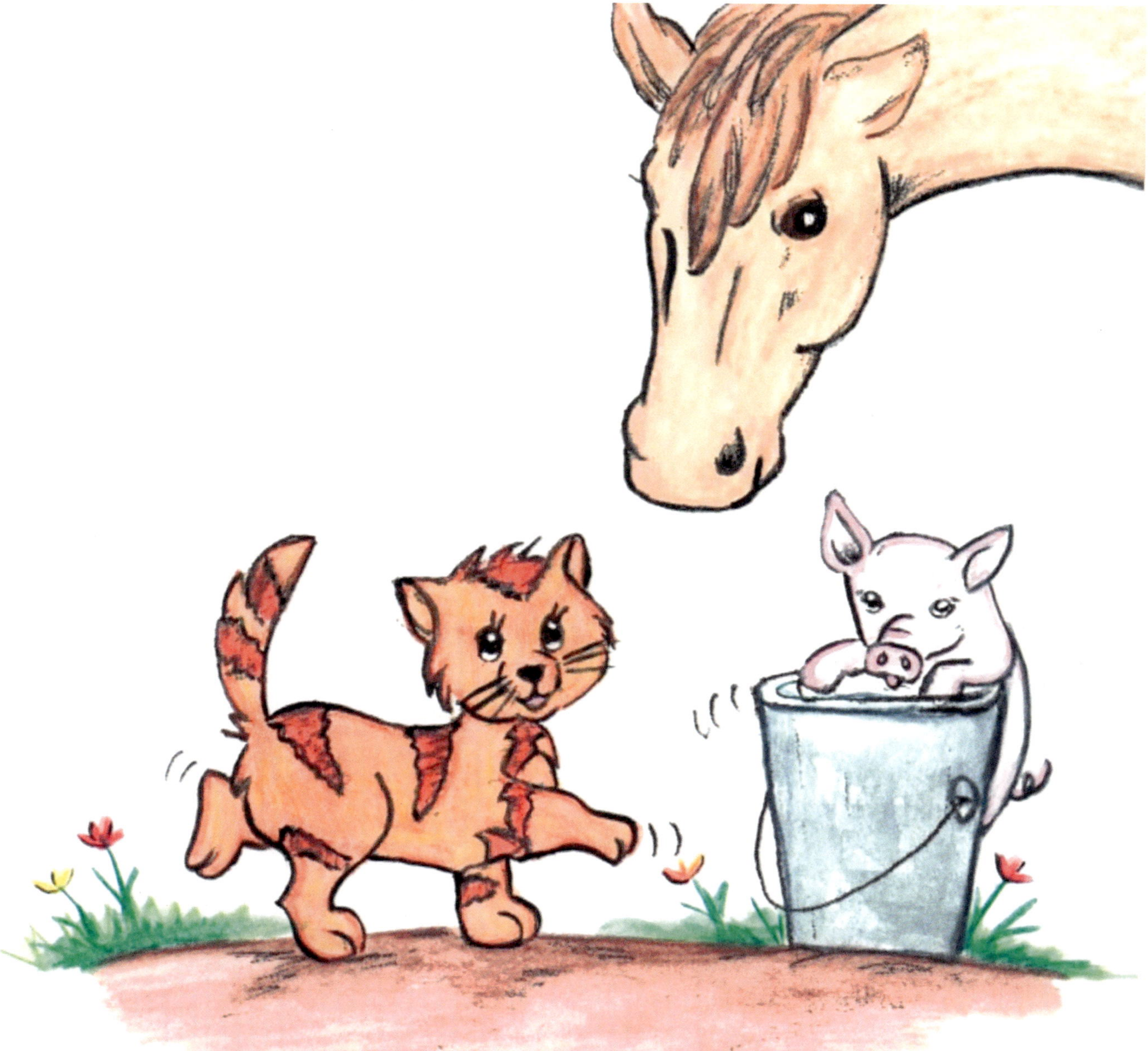

Now you'll know it's a Wampus if it stays out all night.

You're for sure it's a Wampus, in a Wampus cat fight.

Now a Wampus comes red, yellow, grey, or black.

You can tell at a glance by the tail up it's back.

You will know it's a Wampus,

I'm certain of that.

Everyone knows when he's got

A real Wampus cat.

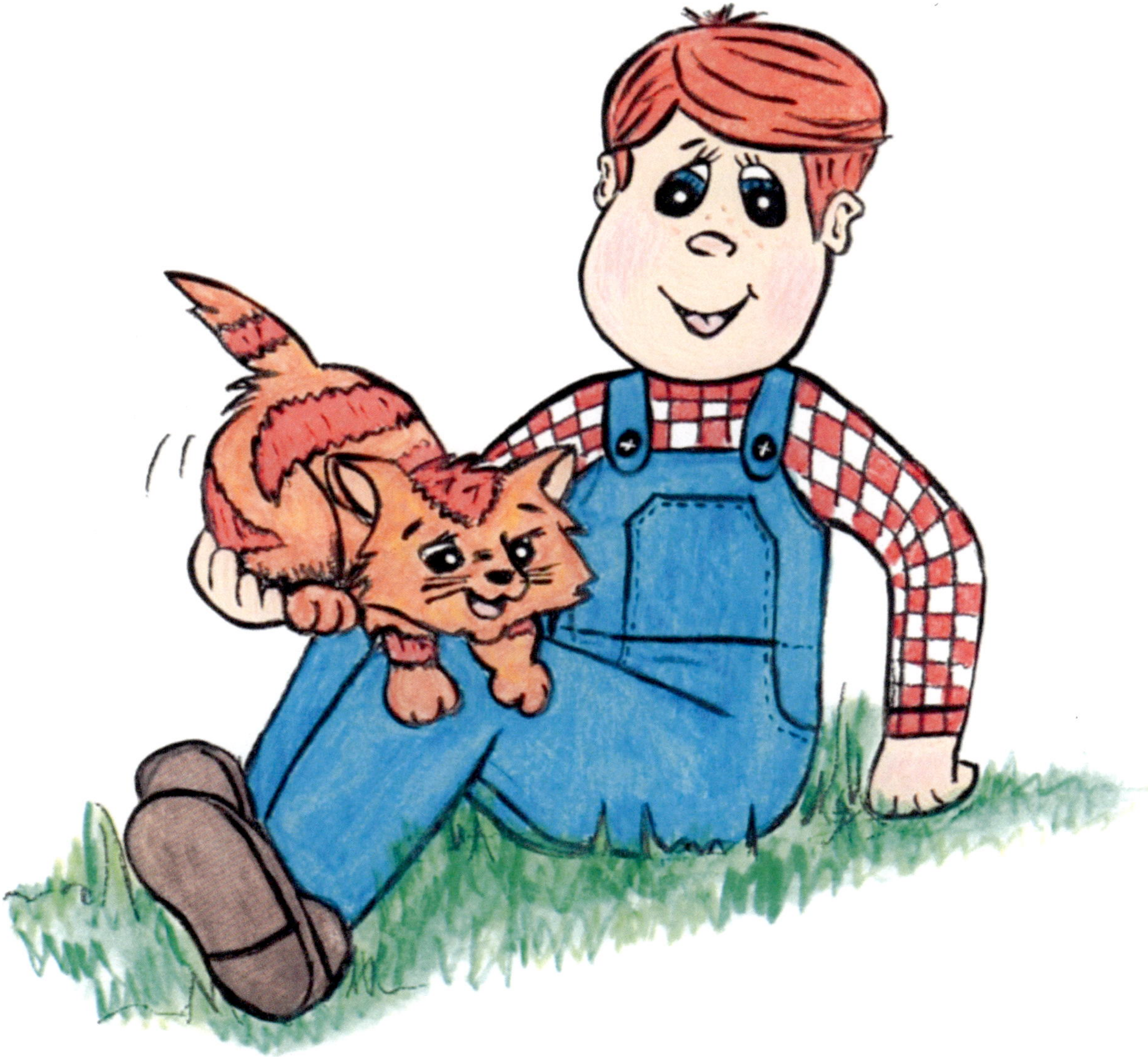

With a smile on his face,

Soon to sleep little Smitty.

Yep!!!

For Sure,

He has a Wampus Kitty!

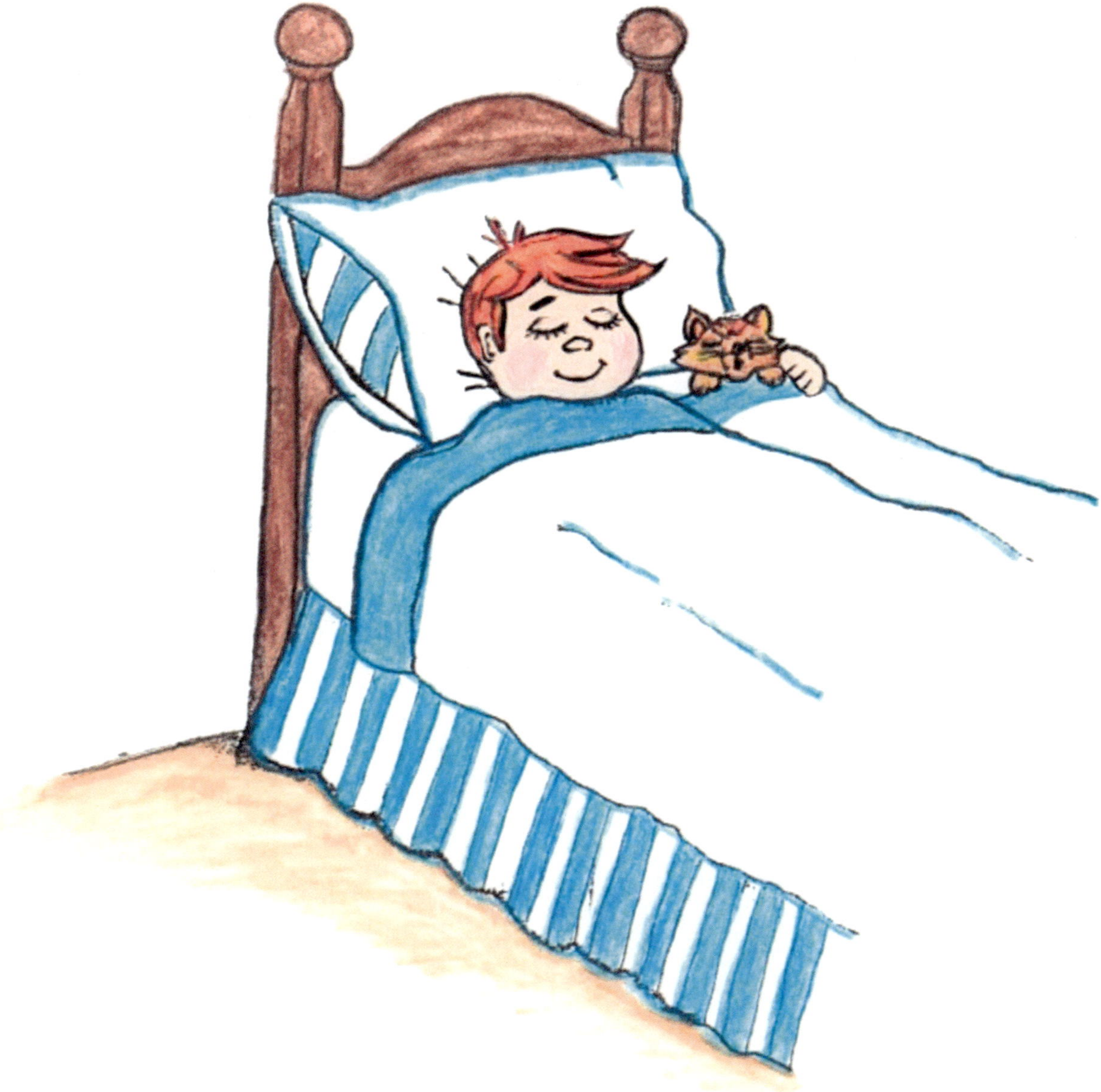

The End

Little Stories from the House of Maxwell

www.BOOKSBYMAXWELL.com

Made in the USA
San Bernardino, CA
09 May 2019